THE PERFECT MURDER

AMANDA MCKINNEY

Storm
PUBLISHING

Ebook ISBN: 978-1-83700-224-5
Paperback ISBN: 978-1-83700-226-9

Cover design: Lisa Horton
Cover images: Shutterstock

Published by Storm Publishing.
For further information, visit:
www.stormpublishing.co

Buried Deception

Trail of Deception

Broken Ridge

The Viper

Mad Women

The Raven's Wife

The Widow of Weeping Pines

Berry Springs

The Woods

The Lake

The Storm

The Fog

The Creek

The Shadow

The Cave

Black Rose Mystery

Devil's Gold

Hatchet Hollow

Tomb's Tale

Evil Eye

Sinister Secrets

Standalones

Lethal Legacy

ONE

TBD – A Thriller

Inspired by the mysterious Quinn and Jacob Lockhart of Bear's Creek.

Written by: Savanna Portman

Lillian

I came here to kill a man.

The moon hangs low in a velvet black autumn sky. Pale light slips through the trees, casting shadows on the damp forest floor beneath my sneakers.

I'm far off the trail now.

I move quickly, sweat dampening my black shirt and leggings. A small hiking pack is strapped to my back, blending into the darkness.

I know this area well, like the back of my hand. The racing, manic thoughts, however, are foreign. They are dark and malicious, worming through my psyche like a virus. I can't stop them, can't shake them away. They are pushing me forward like a heavy hand on my back.

It's time, they whisper.

The scent of charred wood and withering campfire drifts through the trees.

I'm close.

Adrenaline increases my step. I reach back, gloved fingers brushing the side of my pack, verifying the knife is still there.

My heart begins to pound.

I drop low, slinking from tree to tree as I near the cabin.

A strange, almost animal-like focus comes over me. Like a hunter sneaking up on its prey.

As quiet as a deer, I slip through the underbrush, coming up on the backside of the cabin. My senses are on high alert, my ears tuned to every rustle and crack. Over the years, this side of the mountain has become a makeshift encampment with half-hidden shelters made of tarps strung between trees and rope marking property lines. In this part of the woods, you never know who's watching.

Moonlight filters through the clouds, briefly illuminating the small patch of land. Litter covers the ground. Dozens of empty beer bottles and cans. Old wrappers. Plastic bread sleeves. Used needles, charred spoons, wrinkled foil. A pipe.

In the center is a log cabin. A crumbling one-room structure, more ruin than shelter, tucked so deeply into the trees that you'd miss it if not looking for it. The roof has partially caved in on one side and is covered by a faded blue tarp. The chimney leans at an unnatural angle, its cracked bricks scattered around the base like brittle bones. Moss creeps up the sides like mold.

A single window, no larger than a mailbox, is covered with a mildewed floral sheet, so threadbare it flutters like lace in the night breeze.

There is no light inside.

Heart hammering, I maneuver through the litter but slip on a glass bottle. It rolls out from under my sneaker and clanks against another.

I freeze, my eyes rounding as I brace for a response.

None comes.

Once I'm certain my presence remains unknown, I begin again. This time, less harried. Less urgent—less *excited.*

It's time, the voice coos, a jovial hint to her tone. She too is excited.

The time has come.

The wind shifts, carrying a putrid wave of decay. My stomach lurches as I reach into the side pocket of my jacket and retrieve the carving knife.

A ragged snore rattles from the opened window as I pass. Silently, I slip my gloved hand over the door knob.

My grip tightens around the knife in my other hand.

It's time, the voice whispers, louder now.

Driven by some unforeseen but very real thing, I drop to my knees, raise the knife, and stab him through the trench coat.

Though his eyes don't focus, likely from the drugs lingering in his system, he jerks awake and looks directly at me. Shocked.

The emotion hits me like a tidal wave. The release of adrenaline is so severe that I'm suddenly dizzy, heady with a strange, all-consuming rush.

He moans loudly, and I'm enraptured by everything in the moment.

In *awe* of it. The suffering, the *power* I feel.

But as quickly as the emotion arose, a strange, counter-emotion collides with it— sadness.

No, keep going, the voice hisses. *You have to do this.*

Finish it!

When his body finally goes limp, the only sound left is my ragged, shuddering breath.

The knife slips from my fingers, clattering onto scarred hardwood floor.

I stare at the scene in front of me and rock back onto my heels, my chest heaving.

What have I done? Oh God, what have I done?

The sound of movement in the distance spurs me into action. I surge up, but then quickly turn back and pluck the bloody knife from the floor. It's covered in my prints.

Voices, drunk and angry, carry on the distant wind. Someone from the nearby encampment is awake.

I lunge out of the cabin and maneuver through the trash, almost tripping over the makeshift toilet. I can barely balance. I can hardly breathe. The voices in my head grow louder.

What did you do?!

Lillian, what did you do?

Tears blur my vision as I slip into the trees—and run.

TWO

SAVI

The party is too much.

Too many people, too much laughter, too much gold-plated everything. The chandeliers above me drip with crystals, refracting soft light onto the polished marble floors. The towering floral arrangements—roses, hydrangeas, orchids—smell nauseatingly sweet. Everywhere I look, a waiter in a perfectly pressed black-and-white uniform carries a silver tray, offering oysters, caviar, and glasses of champagne.

I should be enjoying this. I should be over the moon.

After all, my debut novel just hit number one on the *New York Times* bestseller list. *Holy Sheet Cake!*, my quirky, food-themed cozy mystery, is being talked about in every book club from here to California. It's thrilling, but at the same time terrifying. Introverts, like myself, enjoy the spotlight about as much as root canals.

In the sudden frenzy of success, my publishing house flew me to New York for a whirlwind three-day trip to discuss another contract, a book tour, and to introduce me to everyone (in the company, it seems) at a lavish party. I spent the day in meetings, shaking dozens of hands, all while sweating bullets from the attention. And in a last-minute twist, my agent booked an event tomorrow. My first-ever speaking engagement—it just sold out.

And yet, as I stand here, clinging to my sparkling water like it's a life raft, all I can think about is how I feel like someone stuffed my socially anxious soul into a sequined jumpsuit and tossed me into the Hunger Games of small talk.

"Darling, you look like you're about to faint—and while that would certainly cause a stir, I do not want you to go viral as the author who collapsed at her own celebration."

I blink and turn toward my agent, Vivienne (Viv) Hearst, who is, as always, larger than life.

Viv is a former editor-turned-literary power player who wears Chanel like it was designed for her specifically. Tonight, she's in a tailored black pantsuit, her silver hair slicked back into a low chignon, her dark, cat-lined eyes scanning the room with the sharpness of a woman who knows her value. In one manicured hand she holds a champagne flute. In the other, a bejeweled vape pen. I contemplate taking a hit of whatever she's puffing on.

"I'm fine," I lie instead, taking another desperate gulp of water.

"You are not fine." Viv leans in, lowering her voice. "You're standing here looking like a deer caught in the headlights of a very expensive Rolls-Royce—and *this* is the moment, my darling. You should be basking. You should be letting people grovel at your feet. Your book just debuted at number one! A debut, thirty-something author just hit it big straight out of the gate. Do you know how many authors would kill for that? Quite literally, in some cases, and I'd know—I represent thriller writers, too."

"Forty-something but who's counting."

She winks. Viv knows exactly how old I am, but I get the impression that to Viv, age is nothing but a number. A very negotiable number.

I sigh. "I know, and I am so grateful. Truly. I just... I don't know how to do this."

"Do what?"

"Any of this." I gesture dramatically around the room. "Be a bestselling author. Be at a party where people keep touching my arm and telling me they 'just adored' my book while I have no idea who they are. Pretend I belong in a room like this."

Viv sighs dramatically, taking my empty glass and replacing it with another sparkling water from a passing waiter's tray. "You belong because I said you belong. And because your readers said you belong. Because the *New York Times* said you belong. And because tomorrow, a ballroom filled with three hundred people—three hundred people who *paid money*—are coming just to hear you speak. And after that, you'll be back in your little sleepy town of Bear's Creek, and you'll be able to unwind. Oh, that reminds me, I had Sarah book an event at the local bookstore the evening you return."

I open my mouth but she cuts me off.

"Don't worry, you're just signing—no speaking. The media will be there, lines will be down the street. It will be fantastic. We have to strike while the iron is hot. And it is, honey. Readers are begging for your next book. Oh, and don't forget, your new editor wants the synopsis ASAP."

I guess now is not the time to tell my agent that what I really want to write next is a psychological thriller. That I have already begun writing this thriller and am so damn excited about it. Cozy mysteries are fun, but my heart is screaming to write *TBD* instead (the current title of said thriller).

"Now," Viv downs her champagne and sets the glass aside, "we are going to walk through this party and you are going to smile that sweet, unassuming small-town girl smile of yours, and you are going to enjoy this moment. Because it's the first time you're experiencing it, and I promise you, nothing—*nothing*—feels quite like the first time you see your name on that list." She winks. "Underneath that big, bold, beautiful number one."

Despite myself, I smile. Because Viv is right. It is an amazing feat and I should be proud. And I am. It's just been a wild ride since, and I've felt suddenly trapped in a world that feels so very foreign.

"You earned this, sweetheart," she presses. "Don't let the glitz and the glam intimidate you."

I glance around the glittering ballroom, the massive floor-to-ceiling windows overlooking Manhattan's skyline, the publishers and editors and media executives sipping their ridiculously over-priced cocktails. These people want to talk to me. Because I wrote a book about a small-town baker turned amateur sleuth who solves a murder over a sabotaged wedding cake, and somehow, that book has resonated with thousands—maybe even millions—of readers. It was even dubbed the "perfect book club pick" by *People* magazine.

I set down my half-finished sparkling water, suddenly feeling the warmth of confidence.

"Alright," I say, linking my arm with Vivienne's. "Let's do this."

She winks, squeezes my hand. "That's my girl."

THREE
JACOB

I can smell the liquor the moment I walk into the house.

"Shit," I mutter, dropping my keys and duty belt onto the console table by the door.

The only light in the house is the glow from the garden lamp-posts outside, slipping through the windows. Beyond that, it's a pitch-black night—three, maybe four in the morning.

I step into the kitchen. As usual, there's no visible sign of overindulgence. No empty bottles left out. No sticky counters. The shot glasses, highball glasses, and wine glasses have all been washed, dried, and placed exactly where they were last night. The liquor bottles are corked and hidden away.

Quinn covers her tracks well.

The headache forming behind my eyes deepens as I head down the breezeway, checking each room as I pass. Years of being a detective means years of unforgiving headaches, and always—*always*—checking my surroundings.

The delayed fatigue from being at a murder/suicide scene all night hits me like a tidal wave. I can't keep up like I used to. It's been decades of answering calls at any given moment, day or night. Decades of bearing witness to the worst things human beings can do to each other. It's wearing on me. My boss has even started planting seeds of retirement in my head. But at almost fifty, I figure I still have at least fifteen years left in me. After all, I'm the only homicide detective in the county. Who would replace me? Who knows these woods like I do?

I stop at the hall mirror. I hardly recognize the face staring back. The gray at my temples is spreading. The stubble on my jaw has more silver than I remember. The lines on my forehead are deeper. My eyes—bloodshot and rimmed with exhaustion—are the worst part. There was a time, not that long ago, when women told me how handsome I was.

I wonder where that time went.

I shake my head and keep moving.

The curtains are drawn in the master bedroom. The television is on, but muted. The bed is still made.

A thin line of light seeps from the half-open bathroom door. The fresh scent of jasmine bubble bath clashes with the sour stench of wine.

"Quinn?" I push the door open.

In a large copper tub, flanked by wall-to-wall windows, Quinn soaks in a sea of bubbles. At least a dozen candles are lit on the vanity, the wax of one dripping onto the marble floor. Quinn's long, skinny arms hang loosely over the sides of the tub. The water is up to her chin.

She's completely still.

For one terrible second, my chest locks up.

Then—a slow blink. The relief is quickly replaced by anger.

"Quinn!" I snap.

Her head slowly lifts from where it was resting against the back of the tub. There's a solid two-second delay before her bloodshot, glassy eyes focus on mine.

"*Dammit*, Quinn." I cross the room. "I told you—I don't like you taking a bath alone when you're drunk."

"I'm not drunk," she slurs, shifting her blank gaze to the arm I'm now gripping.

"And the sun isn't even up for Christ's sake."

"I'm not *drunk*," she slurs again, her head lolling to the side.

That's when I notice a heap of dirty clothes in the corner. Black leggings, black shirt, muddy sneakers. A small black hiking pack. I wonder when the hell Quinn went hiking. Did she take a bottle of wine with her? Has she been up all night?

My jaw clenches.

This is the latest episode of many where Quinn has spiraled into dangerous situations. Once, she blacked out on the chaise longue on the third-floor balcony—mere feet from a thirty-foot drop onto the stone tiles by the pool. Another time, she passed out in the garden during a cold snap. I found her at one in the morning, in the freezing wet dirt, under a tree, wearing nothing but leggings and a sports bra.

I slide my arms under hers, soaking my entire upper body in the process.

"Up."

"No."

I lift again, but she's dead weight.

"Quinn, get up. Get out. I'm tired. I've had a hell of a night, and you're going to pass out in this damn tub and drown to death."

She doesn't move.

Fuming, I bend at the knees and yank her out. She crumbles like a deck of cards onto the now-wet tiles, knocking over the half-empty bottle sitting next to the tub. Red wine spills across the marble, splashing onto me.

For a moment, I want to slap her. A horrible—*horrible*—thought, I know. But I am that mad. That frustrated, that disappointed.

I am that *done* with this.

Forcing down the anger, I toss towels and mats in front of Quinn so that she can get her footing. I pull her up again. She slips and stumbles but eventually rights herself.

Once dry, I hoist her over my shoulder in a fireman's carry and deposit her onto the king-sized bed.

I lean over, forcing myself into her half-lidded line of sight.

"No more baths, okay?"

No response.

I tap her cheek lightly, and speak louder. "Hey. Quinn. You only shower when I'm here. Okay, Quinn? No. More. Baths."

A moan in response. Her eyes are already falling back into her head.

Sighing, I slide a towel under her head and position her on her side, in case she vomits.

I clean the bathroom. Turn off the light.

And then I stand there—arms crossed, exhausted, wet, and stinking of wine—watching her.

Watching until she's completely still.

Until I'm certain she'll remain there for the rest of the day.

FOUR

SAVI

I am going to pass out.

No, seriously. I am about to keel over and die right here in front of three hundred people, all of whom have spent their hard-earned money just to see me. The author of *Holy Sheet Cake!*

The thought makes my stomach churn.

"Stop fidgeting, sweetheart," Viv mutters beside me. She places her perfectly manicured hand on my arm as we wait in the wings of the ballroom stage.

"I'm not fidgeting," I whisper back.

"You're cracking your knuckles like you're about to fistfight Mike Tyson."

I immediately drop my hands, inhaling through my nose. "What if I choke?"

"Darling, if you choke, I will personally set this entire building on fire so no one will ever remember it happened. But you're not going to choke, because you are smart, you are charming, and most importantly, you are the number one bestselling author of *Holy Sheet Cake!*"

She pauses, smoothing her silk scarf like she's about to deliver a eulogy. "Besides, no one here actually cares if you say anything profound. They just want to leave with a signed book."

That makes me feel marginally better.

The event coordinator—a perky woman in a black headset—gestures toward the stage. "Okay, Ms. Portman, you're up!"

The ballroom erupts in applause as my name is announced over the speakers.

Vivienne gives me a little shove. "Go. Be brilliant—be *yourself.*"

I step onto the stage, past the bright floodlights, past the sheer curtains framing the massive book cover banner behind me, and into the blinding attention of three hundred people.

I smile, even though my knees are wobbling.

I take a deep breath as I approach the podium.

"When my publisher told me the event had sold out," I say, "I thought: Oh, cool, my best friend bought a bunch of tickets. But apparently, that's not the case, and there are actual real-life people here who want to talk about my weird, cake-themed murder mysteries. So, thank you all for coming. Though I'm still convinced that *all* of this is some elaborate prank."

Laughter ripples through the room.

Okay. I can do this.

I clear my throat. "So, let's just get the awkward part out of the way—I'm nervous. This is my first-ever book event, and it turns out, writing books and talking about books are two very different skill sets. So, please ignore the red hives that are already working their way up my neck, and try to enjoy what my agent promises will be a mildly entertaining speech."

Another laugh, this one louder. I relax a little.

I glance at the front row, where Viv sits, nodding her approval. She winks.

"Okay, let's begin." I exhale, settling in. "I've been asked many questions since *Holy Sheet Cake!* hit shelves, but the question I get asked the most is why a cozy mystery? Like, I could've written a gritty police procedural, a thriller, heck even a romance. But instead, I chose to write about a quirky baker named Amy with a tendency to stumble into crime scenes while holding a tray of scones."

I pause, tapping my fingers against the podium.

"And the answer is simple. I love cozy mysteries because they take something terrible—like trauma—and wrap it in warmth. There's still crime, still twists, still danger, but at the end of the day, everything is tied up with a neat little bow. Justice is served. The bad guy gets caught. The protagonist bakes another batch of muffins. It's always a warm, happily ever after. I love that predictability. That safety. That certainty."

I swallow, taking a breath, and realize this isn't just a prepared speech meant to entertain, I truly believe what I'm saying. And that steadies me.

"Because life, as we all know, is not a cozy mystery. Sometimes, the bad guy gets away—or is released on some ridiculous technicality. Sometimes, justice never comes. Sometimes, the people you love disappear, and there is no neat little bow to tie around the pain. Writing these books allows me to create a world where everything makes sense. Where I can control everything. Where even in the darkest moments, there is still light. And—based on the number of you who are here today—I think I'm not alone in wanting that kind of story."

A hush settles over the room. Then—thunderous applause.

I blink.

Oh my God. I am *killing* this.

"Okay, enough of my rambling," I say, feeling a tingle of excitement. "I've been told you guys have some questions, so let's get to it. I promise, I'll try to sound like I know what I'm talking about."

The moderator steps up to the mic, and the next hour flies by in a blur of laughter, banter, and actual, real engagement. By the end, my face hurts from smiling, and my nerves have completely disappeared.

As I sign books afterward, people come up to me, gushing about my work, telling me their favorite moments, their favorite characters. And for the first time in this entire whirlwind experience, it hits me—

This isn't just a dream anymore.

This is my life now.

And I cannot allow anything—*anything*—to mess it up.

FIVE
SAVI

Juggling a rainbow-sprinkled frozen yogurt in one hand and a sticky red plastic spoon in the other, I steer with my knee.

It's good to be home, despite being utterly exhausted. I took the red-eye out of New York and landed in the Rocky Mountains just as the sun was rising.

I should go straight home. I should get some rest and prepare for the local signing Viv booked for this evening. Instead, here I am —driving through town in the early morning light, hoping no one notices me. The last thing I want right now is to small-talk with another stranger who feels like they know me.

Bear's Creek is a blink-and-you'll-miss-it town tucked into the foothills of the Wyoming mountains. Over the years, it's transformed into a tourist destination because of its quaint downtown, eclectic shops, and "authentic" Midwestern dining.

The peak of tourist season is autumn—now—when leaf peepers from all over the country flock here to ogle the scenery.

I slow as I cross onto Main Street, taking in the breakfast crowd strolling along the sidewalks. A woman peers at me through the windshield and I quickly look away. Soon, the news will spread— Savanna Portman is back from her big NYC trip. And the questions will begin. The excitement. The congratulations. It's all so overwhelming. I went from an antisocial hermit to small-town celebrity overnight. It's been jarring.

At the light, I close my eyes and drop my head against the headrest. The heater, which hasn't been turned on in months, blows in my face and smells like cheese.

I need to get a new car. The powder-blue minivan that I drive was purchased five years ago—before I was anything special—when my husband, Eric, and I had just begun trying to get pregnant. Now the tragically uncool monstrosity takes up half the garage and serves as nothing more than a daily reminder that instead of being pregnant, I am nothing more than a childless woman driving an eight-person minivan straight into peri-menopause. A reminder that while I have achieved professional success, I have failed miserably at the one thing I really want to achieve.

Being a mom.

I take the road that leads out of town and, within five minutes, am swallowed whole by the dense forest surrounding Bear's Creek. Miles and miles of towering conifers. Shimmering maples. Thick underbrush hugging both sides of the road so tightly the asphalt has cracked in places.

Shoveling a spoonful of frozen yogurt into my mouth, I take a sharp turn up a narrow road that leads to Plummet Heights, a popular hiking trail.

The winding path cuts through a tunnel of trees before dead-ending at a clearing high on the mountain. The parking lot is packed. Mostly tourists, marveling at the rising sun peeking over mountains in the distance.

A young couple, decked out in brand-new hiking gear, reminds me of my husband and I when we were young. They snap selfies next to the caution sign beneath the wooden arch marking the start of the trail.

The sign above them reads:

MOUNTAIN LION SPOTTED IN AREA. PROCEED WITH CAUTION.

I pull into my usual spot at the end of the lot, my tires crunching over brittle brown leaves. Excitement bubbles in my chest—as it always does when I park here. Because this is the only parking spot that offers a glimpse of the lavish, gothic-style mega-mansion hidden in the thickly wooded valley below.

The Lockhart Estate.

There isn't much money in Bear's Creek, but these random mega-mansions aren't uncommon. Wealthy nature-lovers have begun building vacation homes in our area, looking to flee the noise and pollution of the cities. Wyoming and Montana are seeing more and more of this—thanks to the mindfulness movement, a growing trend to unplug, recenter, and actively engage in the present moment.

Jacob and Quinn Lockhart, the owners of the Lockhart Estate, are the postcard-perfect power couple. Influential. Rich. Beautiful. Envied.

Jacob Lockhart is rich because he inherited millions from his grandparents on his fortieth birthday. Jacob is loved because, despite becoming an overnight multi-millionaire, he continued with his job as a county homicide detective. Men respect him. Women adore him.

Quinn, the mysterious lady of the estate, on the other hand, leaves much to the imagination.

I secure my frozen yogurt in the cup holder, then reach under the seat, retrieving my binoculars. After flicking off a sprinkle that had fallen on the strap, I take a quick glance around to confirm no one is watching—not that I need to. No one ever watches a woman in a powder-blue minivan. It's the perfect vehicle to commit a crime. Like spying. (Bordering on stalking.)

Through my binoculars, I take in every intricate detail of the Lockhart Estate.

The structure itself is massive, sprawling across the secluded woodland, with blackened stone walls that tower in stark contrast against the creeping ivy that has begun to reclaim the estate. The architecture is Gothic, with steeply pitched roofs, turrets that stretch toward the sky, and countless arched windows that reflect the rising sun.

To the right of the house, a long stone balcony juts from the second floor, held up by thick, carved corbels that resemble gargoyles. Heavy iron lanterns, flickering dimly with golden light, hang from the eaves. At night they cast eerie, elongated shadows along the cobblestone driveway that snakes toward the grand entrance.

The mansion's many windows reveal glimpses of life inside. Not a single window has curtains—my favorite feature of the home.

I scan from room to room, lingering on the window that I believe leads to the master bathroom. I can just make out the edge of what appears to be a massive copper soaking bathtub.

No Quinn.

Like always—*no Quinn*.

I scoop the last of my melting sprinkles into my mouth and lean back.

For months, I've wondered what she does all day. Where she is.

Despite the Lockharts living in Bear's Creek for years, I have never seen the mysterious Quinn Lockhart in real life.

Not a single time.

SIX

SAVI

I pull into the driveway of my modest three-bedroom, two-bathroom brick home—the same one I've had since long before my book took off. Despite my success, I can't bring myself to consider selling it and upgrading, though I'm not entirely sure why. Maybe it's the quiet comfort of familiarity.

The truth is, while I've received a few hefty payouts from my debut novel, we still have a mortgage to cover and multiple credit cards that we've carried for years. Before all of this—before the book changed everything—my husband and I were living paycheck to paycheck, carefully balancing bills and necessities. And some part of me, even now, isn't quite ready to let go of that life. Also, I know that there is no guarantee that my next book will be a success. That's the thing about this job—it ebbs and flows, and sometimes, it stalls out altogether.

I don't get out right away. Instead, I sit in the garage, staring at the dozen boxes stacked against the wall. We're having a garage sale before winter hits. It was my idea—and I've regretted it every single day since.

Half the boxes are still unopened, waiting to be sifted through. The other half are tipped over, spilling clothes and random items onto the concrete floor. Knickknacks litter the space like little soldiers. Junk is everywhere. An old toaster oven, an ice machine, an elliptical I used for exactly one week before deciding my stride wasn't wide enough for whatever ogre it was built for.

When I finally make it into the house, the first thing I do is kick off my flats with a groan. Aging is cruel. Along with zero libido and the emergence of facial hair, bunions decided to show up at forty.

I drop my luggage by the door.

The house is quiet.

Sunlight filters through dirty windows, pooling onto the hardwood floors. As I pass, dust particles sparkle in my wake, and I make a mental note to call around about housekeeping. Certainly I can afford housekeeping now.

My gaze lands on the framed photo of me and Eric at the beach. In the picture, he's cradling me in his arms, like a groom crossing the threshold of our first home together. My head is tilted back, mid-laugh.

I miss him.

Eric isn't expected home for a few more days, though he often surprises me with an early arrival.

When I married a long-haul trucker, I had no idea how lonely it would be. He's gone for four—sometimes six—weeks at a time. Home for two, sometimes less. Then on the road again. Today, though, it feels like I haven't seen him in five years.

I slide a leftover chicken spaghetti casserole into the oven and start the dishwasher.

After making a cup of chai tea, I head to the master bedroom, stripping out of my jeans and blouse. My thoughts are already back on work and the next cozy mystery I'm supposed to be outlining. I need to deliver the synopsis to my editor ASAP—his words exactly.

There was a time when my writing process looked like a carefully crafted murder board in a detective movie. Index cards, color-coded by chapter. Plot points tacked onto cork boards. Sticky notes trailing across my wall like neon breadcrumbs. I even had a label maker.

Now?

Now my pastel-colored index cards are scattered across the corner of the bedroom floor in chaotic clusters. A few have coffee rings on them. One is stuck to the bottom of a random sock under the desk.

I drop to my knees in the middle of it all and try to make sense of what I've written.

Each card holds a scene, a line of dialogue, or an idea that felt like a stroke of brilliance when I jotted it down at two in the morning. Now, in the full, unflattering light of day, I can't tell if I'm outlining a cozy mystery or mapping out the final days of my sanity.

The cards are supposed to be organized in three acts, marked by subplot and character arc. But somewhere between Act One and the Midpoint Twist, the system unraveled into a mess of jumbled half-thoughts.

What if the killer is actually the cat? and *Does the corpse really need to be found in the bakery freezer?*

I take a deep breath. I can't do this right now. So, I grab my laptop and check my email.

Big mistake.

Fifty-two unread emails, twelve flagged as urgent, three from my publicist marked '**[FOLLOW UP]**', and one from my agent that just says '**??**' in the subject line.

I open Instagram next.

The first thing I see is a re-posted photo of myself holding a signed copy of *Holy Sheet Cake!*, beaming like I haven't a care in the world. But I can see right through it. The smile is frozen, the kind that starts to ache after twenty takes. My dirty hair is pinned in the back to fake volume on top, and while the silk blouse says 'polished author', just below the camera's frame I'm wearing baggy sweatpants and fuzzy slippers. The selfie stand I used to take the photo is propped on a box of Thin Mints, angled just right to capture what, at the time, I thought was a decent picture.

My publicist convinced me to open these accounts—Instagram, Twitter (I refuse to call it X), and a Facebook author page where I have accumulated a suspiciously large following of middle-aged conservative white men.

I wrinkle my nose at the image of myself. I look tired and weirdly swollen, and my nose looks big.

Do I have a big nose? Is it possible I've gone through life with a cartoon beak on my face and no one—*not a single person*—told me?

Before long, I am Googling *photo editing apps that smooth skin,* then get distracted by a YouTube video called *How to Pose in Selfies.*

I scribble on a notecard:

Practice posing later this week.

It hits me then, between the exhaustion of traveling and the stress of deadlines—this is unsustainable. I can't write books, go on tours, give charming interviews, and master the fine art of filtered selfies. I can't be two people at once: the composed author and the woman behind the camera, that feels like one epic hot mess.

The anxiety starts to press in, when, thankfully I'm distracted by the garage door opening and slamming shut.

SEVEN

SAVI

"Yum! I'm starved!" Katie's voice echoes down the hall. She must have smelled the casserole bubbling away in the oven.

I hear one heel, two, drop onto the tiled floor, exactly where my flats and luggage still sit. Then footsteps, the thud of a handbag being tossed onto the couch as she passes the living room, and the shedding of clothes as she makes her way down the hall.

Finally Katie arrives at my bedroom door.

Her long brown hair is windblown from driving with her car windows down—a feeble attempt to mask the lingering scent of her *"car cigarette."* She calls it that because that's the only place she'll smoke them. Just like the only place she'll eat dessert is in the bathtub. Wine, though? She'll drink that anywhere.

Katie is my best friend and, by definition, a functioning alcoholic. I love her dearly.

She's also: A pastry chef (amateur, but don't tell her that). A serial dater (of deeply questionable men). A karaoke star (in her own mind). And, lastly, completely unapologetic about her curvy body (my favorite thing about her).

Most recently, Katie has become a roommate after Eric urged her to move into the spare room to keep me company while he was away. Some days, I don't know what I'd do without her.

Katie lunges into the room, drops to her knees where I'm still sitting on the floor surrounded by index cards, and wraps her arms around me.

"Welcome home!"

I inhale the comforting scent of my best friend, cigarette and all.

"Tell me *everything*." She pulls back, gripping my shoulders. She's lit with excitement.

"I already did," I laugh. "We talked and texted like a million times a day while I was gone."

"I know but I want to hear it all again. I am so, *so* proud of you. Get up though, my knees can't take this."

We pull each other off the floor and I dramatically fling myself onto the bed. "Oh, girl, it was so *exhausting*."

Katie, now holding a bottle of wine and a glass that magically appeared from nowhere, sinks onto the edge of the bed and pours herself a drink. "I'm sure it was! I wish you would have let me come. I really wanted to be there for you."

"I know, and thank you for offering to go, but you've got work, and besides, I had my agent and publicist with me at all times. Trust me—I was *never* alone."

I tell her everything. *Again.* Emphasizing how uncomfortable it all is and how sometimes I feel like I'm playing a character in my own life. Ironic, I know. As always, Kat offers all the right words, at all the right moments.

After she leaves, I stare at the ceiling fan above my bed, its slow rotation hypnotic, rhythmic, almost soothing if not for the sharp edge of unease sitting just beneath my skin. My thoughts, as they always do, drift to the mysterious Jacob and Quinn Lockhart.

This new (secret) manuscript I'm writing—the one that's clawing its way out of me—is dark and messy and everything my cozies aren't.

It all swirls around one question.

Where is Quinn Lockhart?

What if she's locked in a room somewhere inside that sprawling estate, and no one even knows?

Or worse.

What if she's dead?

He could do it, you know. Cover it up. Clean up the evidence. He is the police, after all. The one who'd be called if there were a report. The one who writes the reports.

And that's what gnaws at me. The not-knowing. The aching, gnawing curiosity that feels less like a question and more like an obsession.

Later, after Katie has settled in to watch her trashy reality television, I sit at my computer desk, tucked into the corner of the bedroom. (Surrounded by mounds of manic index cards.)

I open the file entitled TBD, otherwise known as my dark twisted thriller.

I glance over my shoulder, then back at the yet-to-be-named manuscript. At the fictional account of the narrative that plays in my head over and over again. The story of the mysterious Jacob and Quinn Lockhart.

In my book, she's Lillian. He's Andrew. (Because I can't give them their real names, right?)

Lillian and Andrew.

The perfect couple.

Or are they?

I take a sip of tea, set my fingers on the keyboard.

And pick up where I left off.

EIGHT

TBD – A Thriller

Inspired by the mysterious Quinn and Jacob Lockhart of Bear's Creek.

Written by: Savanna Portman

Lillian

I stand beneath the arched doorway of the study, wearing nothing but a pair of six-inch red patent heels.

Andrew sits in front of a roaring fire, his broad shoulders hunched, the glow flickering across the sharp angles of his face. Leather-bound books tower behind him. Shadows stretch across the dark stone walls. He looks like something from an old noir film, whiskey in one hand, a smoldering cigar in the other.

Outside, rain lashes the windows, streaking down the glass in frantic, twisting rivulets. Lightning pops. Thunder rolls in moments later.

Andrew senses me, as he always does. Like a panther, my detective husband doesn't need to see or hear something coming—he simply feels it.

There's no greeting when I step into the room. No excitement.

Instead, he takes a moment, as if gathering himself before slowly turning his head.

When he sees me, he closes his eyes, shakes his head, and turns back to the fire.

"You're drunk, Lillian. Go to bed."

"I'm not drunk." My heels wobble as I step forward.

Andrew doesn't even look at me.

He knows I'm lying. He always does. Sometimes it feels like my husband is omnipresent—his awareness stretching into every corner of this house. Always watching. Always finding me.

But there are some secrets he will never, ever know.

I stumble forward.

Andrew, growing more annoyed, mutters, "I said, go to bed."

"Not until you fuck me."

Nothing. Not even a flicker of emotion. I might as well have told him I murdered someone. The reaction would've been the same.

It's not that Andrew doesn't care—it's that he's become bored and detached from this loveless marriage we live in.

Frustrated and emboldened by the alcohol, I step in front of the fire, in front of my husband, stark raving naked. Feigning confidence, I force myself to stand tall and lift my chin. The heat from the fire washes over my backside.

"Look at me," I snap.

"No."

"Why?"

Releasing a growl of exasperation, Andrew pushes off the leather chair. He retreats to the corner of the room, putting as much distance between me and him as possible.

Enraged (and mildly embarrassed), I advance, but teeter on my heels, and eventually fall. I catch myself on the edge of the chair before collapsing into it.

"Dammit!" Andrew rushes over to help.

I swat him away. My cheeks burn.

With a snarl, I rip off one shoe and hurl it into the fire.

The second follows.

"Lillian, *stop*."

"No!" I surge to my feet, more steady now that I'm barefoot. "We haven't had sex since—I don't even remember when!" I gesture to my naked body, voice pitching higher. "I put on makeup, did my hair; I'm naked for Christ's sake—I even gave you time to unwind!"

Andrew scrubs his hands over his face.

"What's wrong with me?" I scream, and a little warning bell goes off somewhere deep inside my subconscious.

Stop, Lillian.

You're being craaazy.

Agaiiin.

"I can't do this right now." Andrew shoulders past me, storming toward the door.

I rush after him, stopping just short of the threshold, gripping the doorframe for support.

I watch my husband stomp up the grand staircase. The chandelier overhead glows like a constellation, reflecting off his dark hair.

When he disappears into the shadows, I turn back to the fireplace, staring at my brand-new Louboutins ablaze in the flames.

I could throw myself into the fire. Maybe that would get his attention.

Tears roll down my cheeks, yet my jaw clenches in anger. And once again, I give myself the same, tired pep talk that I have given so many times before.

I will not live this way. I will not live in a loveless home. I am better than this.

I deserve better than this.

Warring with my desire to leave and the fact I know I won't, I spin into an emotional frenzy and run up the stairs, forcing myself forward with each step. Maybe if I leave for a few nights, he'll miss me. Maybe then he'll finally know how serious I am that we need to make big changes in our marriage.

Tears streaming down my face, I storm into the walk-in closet and yank a cashmere sweater off the hanger, sending it flipping off the hook and into the air. It clatters to the floor as I pull on matching lounge pants. Lastly, a pair of brown, leather hiking boots.

"Fuck him," I spit through quivering lips, more to embolden myself than anything. *Don't stop now, Lillian,* I might as well be saying.

Once back downstairs, I secure my Saint Laurent crossbody, and, after a quick glance over my shoulder, I tiptoe to the fridge. Stretching into the small space between the backside of the fridge and the wall, I find the magnetic lockbox that hides the key fob to my car. The lockbox my husband thinks I don't know about.

I slip out the door and jump into my Audi. I have absolutely no idea where I'm going; I just know that I want to be gone. No—that I want *him* to know I'm gone.

The garage door opens. The roar of the rain fills the space.

I slide into the Audi, heart pounding, hands shaking. I slam the car into reverse, tires skidding over the wet pavement—

And scream.

Andrew stands in the driveway behind me, his tall silhouette bathed in red from the taillights. Rain pounds his shoulders. His fists are clenched at his sides.

Chest heaving, we stare at each other through the rearview mirror.

For a split second, a terrible thought crosses my mind—

Run him over.

I shudder, surprised I could even have a heinous thought like that.

I put the car into drive, roll forward.

Dripping wet, Andrew steps beside the driver side door and extends his palm.

I roll down the window and drop the key fob into his hand.

"You are never, *ever* to leave this house without my permission." He growls. "You know that, Lillian."

I lower my gaze.

"Yes," I whisper. "I do know that."

NINE
SAVI

The bookstore event went off without a hitch. Katie—my assistant, as she introduced herself to everyone—stood by my side the entire time. I signed books and didn't even have to speak to the media.

Now we're home. The house is quiet, save for the faint hum of the refrigerator and the occasional groan of the heating vents.

It's almost eleven o'clock. I should be sleeping, but instead, I'm here. Sitting at my desk, bathed in the pale glow of my laptop screen, working on the cozy mystery synopsis that is due to my editor "ASAP."

My tea has gone cold. I pick it up anyway, cradling the mug in both hands, inhaling the faint scent of chai and honey. It's meant to be soothing, but my nerves are wired.

The cursor blinks at me. Taunting, because it knows I won't leave. It knows I need to lose myself in someone else's life.

An email pops up.

Subject: Great News!

Vivienne Hearst.
God help me.
I groan out loud before I even open the email, because anytime

Vivienne uses the words "Great news," it usually includes a commitment on my end. And I feel like I'm already holding my new career together with rubber bands and lies.

I click it open.

How does being on the hottest morning show in the country sound?!

My stomach drops to the floor. My heart vaults into my throat and starts thumping.

The email continues:

The *It's A Great Day* show wants you for their Most Anticipated Winter Reads segment! You'd pick five books you love (not your own, obviously), give a cute little synopsis of each, and share why readers will love them—with a blanket and hot cocoa perhaps? Think cozy, think charming, think—YOU! Maybe even throw in a pun about your "baking" books? ;) Just a thought!

Oh, and it's in NYC, so they'll fly you up. Think about it and let me know by the end of the week. And don't forget to send your cozy synopsis to Eliot ASAP.

Kisses, Viv

I gape at the screen.

Live. Cameras. Lights. Microphones shoved in my face. Me, sweating through my thong, pretending like I belong.

My palms are damp. My face is on fire.

This email—an email alone—is sending me into a borderline panic attack.

What the hell is wrong with me?

Why am I not excited? This is every author's dream.

Since my book hit the list, I've felt like I've been on a treadmill I didn't sign up for—running faster and faster, smiling harder, saying yes to everything, nodding along while people shove makeup on my face and tell me I'm "a brand now." I'm not a brand. Some days I feel like I'm barely a person.

Get a grip, Savi.

I press my hand to my chest, trying to slow my pulse. I'm officially suffocating inside my own success. And the worst part? I can't really talk to anyone about it. Because this is what I *wanted,* right?

Right?

My eyes flick back to the email.

Think about it and let me know by the end of the week.

Yeah, Viv. Let me just pencil in a full-blown identity collapse between now and Friday.

I click out of the email like it's a poisonous thing and stare at my files.

TBD.

Why is it the only time I feel like *me* anymore is when I'm writing about murder? And even then, sometimes it feels like I'm not the one writing at all. Instead it's the little voice in my head.

Keep writing, Savi.

Just keep writing.

Footsteps creak down the hallway. Katie.

I slam shut the laptop, but then yank it open again, pretending I'm deep in some productive train of thought. My fingers land on the keys. I type nonsense.

asljdfhalwiefhwefhlkjh

"Savi?"

Fingers still on the keyboard, I turn to see my best friend leaning against the doorframe, arms crossed, watching me. She's in her usual ratty T-shirt and pajama shorts, hair piled into a messy bun. Wine glass in hand, of course.

I cock a brow. "Am I in trouble, Mother?"

"That depends, darling," she mocks. "Did you take your sleeping pill?"

I sigh, sinking back in my chair.

Here we go.

"Katie—"

"Nope." She pushes off the doorframe, stepping into the room. "That's not an answer."

I close my laptop halfway. Not all the way—just enough to let her know I'm sort of listening.

"I'll take it in a bit," I promise.

Katie huffs, setting her wine glass on my nightstand.

"You always say that," she mutters, reaching for the pill bottle next to my lamp. She shakes it, the pills rattling against plastic. "And then you sit here all night, typing until your eyes bleed, and suffer a terrible migraine tomorrow."

I should be annoyed. I should tell her I don't need a babysitter. But the truth is, I'm grateful that I have a friend who cares enough to keep track of me, to check in, to make sure I don't just fade into my own routine of sleepless self-destruction.

Katie softens as she looks at me. "Come on," she says, a little gentler now. "Take it."

I hesitate. Not because I don't want to sleep. But because I hate that I *need* something to make it happen. That I need so many different pills for sleep and migraines.

Katie gently shakes the bottle when I hesitate. "You know what happens if you don't," she says.

"I know. I will, I promise."

Katie nods approvingly, like she's just convinced a child to eat their vegetables.

She sets down the bottle, grabs her wine glass, and heads for the door.

"Good girl," she teases over her shoulder.

I roll my eyes. "I hate you."

"Love you too, babe."

She disappears down the hall, her footsteps fading.

I sit there for a while, staring at the pill bottle, before finally opening my laptop again.

I click into *TBD*, where the Lockharts live.

Where they wait.

For me to tell their whole story.

On a deep exhale, I begin to write. I write, and write, and write—draining out the stress, slipping out of this world and into another. The words pour out of me, relentless. I'm typing so fast my fingertips hurt.

It almost feels like I'm watching from above—some part of me detached, hovering, observing the scene unfold with violent clarity.

And it feels good.

It feels *so* good to disappear. To leave this world behind for one I can control. One where everything makes sense.

TEN

JACOB

My phone dings.

I slide my highball glass onto the table, next to the half-drunk pint of bourbon, then glance at the clock. Midnight.

I pick up my phone and see one new text from Selma.

I can't sleep.

I lift my socked feet off the ottoman, plant them on the floor, and lean forward, cupping the phone with both hands.

I stare at the text. At her name. Selma—my beautiful Selma.

Me either.

My gaze shifts to the dwindling flames in the fireplace, waiting for her response.

It comes a minute later.

I'm sorry you can't sleep.

Me too.

Come over.

I can't.

I understand.

I grab my glass. When I realize it's empty, I slam it down and take a long pull straight from the bottle instead.

The fire pops and hisses angrily—a visual representation of how I feel inside.

I glance at the clock again.

I can't go out now. I should be sleeping, like other normal human beings. Instead, my mind is unraveling, knotted with anxiety since walking in on Quinn nearly passed out in the bathtub.

Why do I put up with this?

Because you have to.

"An impossible situation," I mutter, growing angrier.

Yes, it is... and you have needs, too.

"Fuck it." I surge to a stance.

After locking the bourbon back in the hidden safe inside the bookshelves, I smother the fire.

Ten minutes later, I pull into the cracked pavement of Plummet Heights Apartments.

The night is bone-chilling cold, the air unnervingly still as I quietly latch the door of my truck.

My breath comes out in puffs of clouds as I walk up the concrete steps to unit number seven.

Before I can knock, Selma opens the door. Her dark eyes—though puffy with lack of sleep—twinkle under the porch light.

Seeing her sends a rush of warmth over my body, and instantly, it seems, the knots in my shoulders relax. The pounding in my head eases.

She's wearing the red silk robe I gifted her six months ago for her birthday. Under it, I know she's naked.

"Come in," she whispers, her sultry, husky voice driving me wild.

Before the door even latches, we are in each other's arms. Kissing wildly. Shedding clothes. Threading fingers through hair.

We make love right there, on the floor, next to the front door.

For a long time after, we say nothing. Just lay there, wrapped in the warmth of each other's arms. Her head lays on my chest, in the little nook next to my shoulder. She fits perfectly there, like she was made for it. Like we were made for each other.

As my fingers comb through her long, black hair, I breathe in the soft floral scent and think: I never want to leave. Her arms, this place, this floor. I want to freeze this moment and stay in it forever.

If only it were that simple.

"Is Quinn getting worse?" Selma finally speaks, addressing the elephant in the room.

"Yes." I swallow deeply. "Worse than I've ever seen her."

Selma lifts her head from my chest. Her dark brows pull together, concerned. "Jacob."

"I know."

I close my eyes and grit my teeth.

God, I just want it to go away.

All of it.

"But she's had these manic episodes before, right? For years?"

"Yes, but not like this. And never this close together. It's escalating dramatically. More than ever."

"What's triggered it?"

"I don't know." I exhale, frustrated. "I don't know what to do."

"Where is she getting the booze? You lock yours up, right?"

"Yes, and I don't know that either. I think she buys it when she goes into town for groceries."

Selma frowns. "Can you call the manager at the liquor store?"

"And tell him what? To deny her purchase or ban her from the store? Can you imagine how she'd react?"

"And she'd find it somewhere else anyway," Selma murmurs, and I nod.

A moment stretches between us.

I say, "I started logging my bottles—marking how much is in each one at the end of the night, in case she somehow found my stash. But she hasn't." I shake my head. "I even thought about throwing it all out. Stopping drinking myself."

Selma trails her fingertips down my forearm. "You've done that before."

"Yes. I've quit drinking for Quinn a dozen times, and *dammit* if it changed anything. She still gets drunk. And, you know what? I miss my nightly bourbon. Why should I have to give up so much?"

Selma's fingers tighten over my arm. "I'm so sorry, Jacob."

"No." I gently lay Selma on her back and lean over her. I cup her face in my hands, and stare into the eyes of the woman I love. The woman who owns not a piece of my heart—but the whole damn thing.

"I'm sorry *for you*." I swallow hard. "I'm sorry you have to deal with this. With me. Like this. With Quinn. With everything."

Selma shakes her head, pressing her hands over mine.

"Honey, I'm not going anywhere." She snuggles closer. "I'm here for the long haul. You know that."

My throat tightens. "And that's why I love you."

Tears fill her eyes.

"I love you so, so much, Selma."

More than anyone.

More than anything.

"Until the day I die, I will love you with everything I have to give."

ELEVEN

TBD – A Thriller

Inspired by the mysterious Quinn and Jacob Lockhart of Bear's Creek.

Written by: Savanna Portman

Lillian

Lines of sunlight sneak through the shutters, stretching across the comforter. One sunbeam sits directly on my face, burning my eyes as I blink them open. Groaning, I swat at the cursed sun.

I am so hungover that for a moment, I wonder if it could be something more. If it's possible I have food poisoning.

But of course I don't have food poisoning. After all, I only ingested a bowl of organic oatmeal, a banana, a protein shake, and two bottles of wine yesterday.

I don't need to look at the clock to confirm it's mid-morning.

My husband, Andrew, is hours into his job as homicide detective—the love of his life—after probably tiptoeing around me while getting ready (eons ago), silently berating me for sleeping in.

My phone vibrates on the nightstand.

Eyes squeezed shut, I roll over, flap my hand around the nightstand until I find it. I rip it off the charger, sending the wire swinging against the table.

Squinting, I study the screen.

Three missed calls. Five text messages.

That's strange.

I click through the texts.

"Oh *shit*."

I sit up too fast. A wave of nausea crashes into me. I drop the phone onto the comforter and lurch out of bed, barely making it to the toilet before all hell breaks loose.

I vomit twice more before it's over.

Exactly how much did I drink last night? I replay the evening in my head. After confronting my husband, naked, demanding he have sex with me, then storming out of the house, then Andrew catching me, and then taking my car keys, I *thought* I went straight to bed (as he demanded).

I *thought* I fell asleep.

Did I drink more?

Feeling like death, I drag myself back to bed, back to my phone.

Where was I?

Oh yes.

Bypassing the texts, I click into the latest voicemail, sent one hour ago.

Might as well get straight to the point.

Maddie's nasal, high-pitched, rich-girl voice comes through the speaker:

"Hey Lillian, it's Maddie. We've called and texted several times this morning but haven't been able to get ahold of you.

"You might have forgotten, but today is the big Fill the Turkey event at the Cara Center. You signed up to lead the event—you know, to ensure those less fortunate than us have something to eat on Thanksgiving next month?"

(She pauses—just long enough to ensure I catch the jab. Bitch, I can feel it through the damn phone.)

"So, uh, listen. We had a quick meeting this morning, and we've decided to release you of your duties as vice chair committee.

"No need to call back or attend any future meetings. I've already assigned Ashlee the role.

"We wish you all the best! God bless!"

My empty stomach drops.

Did I just get *fired?* Can you even be fired from volunteering?

Shame heats my cheeks as I sit there. Stinking of booze and sweat. In my king-sized bed. Under my imported silk sheets. Beneath my four-thousand-dollar duvet.

I have just been fired from *volunteer* work. Is that even a thing?

Oh God. What will Andrew say? He's already disappointed in me—for just breathing it seems.

Tears fill my eyes.

I am disgusted with myself. With my inability to stop drinking. With my inability to be the sophisticated, proper woman my husband wishes I were. With my inability to control my impulses.

Most of all, I am disgusted with *this*—my pitiful self-loathing.

I hurl the phone across the room.

"I *hate* myself," I mutter through gritted teeth, ripping off the comforter.

I stand, staggered by another dip in my stomach. Again, I run to the bathroom and throw up.

And again.

Thirty minutes later, I'm still sitting on the bathroom floor, wet wash-cloth in hand, when the thought hits me—

When was my last period?

I frown, scanning my memory. I can't remember.

I peel myself off the cold tiles, stumbling across the room to where I threw my phone.

My hands tremble as I unlock the screen. I open the period tracking app I downloaded last year. The highlighted date glares back at me.

It's been ten weeks since my last period.

"Oh my God."

My heart begins to pound.

I whirl around, ripping open the bathroom cabinet. I know I have one pregnancy test leftover from a scare last year. I snatch it, my fingers shaking as I rip open the box.

I take the test.

Three minutes later—

I stare at the two thick lines.

For a moment, everything slows. The hum of the bathroom fan fades, the drip of the faucet silences, even my heartbeat stalls in my chest.

I stumble backward, sinking to the edge of the bathtub.

Tears spring to my eyes—an emotional cocktail of shock, fear, wonder.

I press a washcloth to my mouth, gaping at the test.

I am pregnant.

TWELVE

SAVI

It's midnight, the time of night where you feel completely alone. The bottle of sleeping pills sit next to me, unopened. I haven't taken one yet. Instead, I'm just lying here, tracing the comforter with my thumb, staring up at the ceiling.

Outside, a frigid wind pushes through the trees, soft and slow like a lullaby. The moonlight filters through my curtains, casting pale streaks across the wall.

I cried for over an hour. Writing about my main character, Lillian, discovering she is pregnant, has triggered something in me. I guess because I want that so badly. There's a soft knock on my bedroom door, followed by the quiet creak as it opens. Katie's voice floats in, low and gentle.

"I thought I heard you crying."

I sit up slightly, swiping at my cheeks, but she doesn't turn on the light. She doesn't ask what's wrong, because she knows there are times to ask, and times to not. Instead, she just crosses the room, slips off her slippers, and sinks onto the bed.

She looks down at me, and I wonder if she notices my swollen eyes.

"Thank you," I whisper.

She smiles, climbs into bed beside me. "I'll just lay with you until you fall asleep," she whispers, grabbing the afghan I keep at the foot of the bed and pulling it up to her chin.

We lie there in silence, staring up at the ceiling, our shoulders barely touching.

And just like that, I'm pulled back to the moment our friendship was sealed, in the corner booth of a dive bar with sticky floors and dollar beer. It was the first time Katie opened up to me.

It was five years ago.

We were at Malone's, a little dive bar off Main. A blues band played in the corner, slow and gritty. Katie and I sat in a booth near the back. Her drink—something amber and strong—sweated in her hand. Mine was just water.

Katie looked different that night. Her usual spark had dimmed. She was quieter than usual. Her laughter forced, her focus drifting.

"What's going on?" I asked, stirring my straw. "You seem off."

"It's my mom's birthday," she said finally. "She would've been eighty today. That's a big one."

Katie rarely talked about her mom, so I stayed quiet, letting her take her time.

"She was my best friend," she went on, her voice low and thoughtful. "My whole damn world, you know? We were always together. Movie nights, road trips, even dumb little errands. We were more like sisters than mother and daughter."

I could see the warmth in her face when she said it. And the pain that followed.

"Then she got sick. Dementia. And it was like both our worlds came tumbling down. At first it was small stuff—forgetting names, misplacing things. But then it got worse. A lot worse." She looked down into her glass, her fingers tightening. "I quit my job to take care of her full-time. Everyone said I was crazy, but I didn't care. I couldn't let her go through that alone." Her eyes shimmered with unshed tears. "It's a really awful disease, Savi. Like, terrible."

The band kept playing, slow and heavy, like the air between us.

"Eventually, she forgot who I was. Sometimes she'd scream at me. Other times she'd cry and cling to me like a child. I'd bathe her, feed her, clean up after her when she had accidents. It was brutal. Watching the person you love disappear piece by piece. Like someone was erasing her from the inside out."

She swallowed deeply, doing everything she could not to cry. It broke my heart.

"And when she died," she said quietly, "I thought I'd feel relief. Isn't that awful? But I was just so tired. So worn down. But then, the relief never came. Just more silence. And a whole lot of guilt."

She finally looked up at me, her voice cracking. "And it was after that that my drinking picked up. I just kind of felt aimless— like I was just floating through this world with no real purpose. The first job I took after that was awful, so I quit. Same with the second one, so I quit. And now here I am. Still drunk, still going through jobs like I'm a teenager. I always feel... restless. Like I'm chasing something I can't name."

Tears welled in my eyes.

"But then I met you," she added with a small, sad smile. "And it's like... I don't know. Like I had a sister again, a soulmate," she reached over and grabbed my hand, "like I'm able to help someone again. You make me feel value again. Our friendship has given me purpose again."

I squeezed her hand. We didn't say anything else for a while. We just sat there, letting the music carry us, our shared silence more comforting than any words could've been.

THIRTEEN

SAVI

I wake up like someone just punched me in the face.

My chest is heaving. My skin sweaty.

The sheets are tangled around me like ropes.

I blink rapidly into the dark, my pulse thundering in my ears.

It was just a dream.

A nightmare.

The same one I've had over and over again: a man collapsing in front of me, clutching his chest. Someone I love, but someone who has no face. In the dream, I try to move toward him, but my feet never work. I scream, but no sound comes out. He falls, and I watch him die of a heart attack.

I press the heels of my hands to my eyes, trying to scrub away the image, but it lingers like smoke in the corners of my mind. No matter how hard I try, I can't bring the man's face into focus.

I reach for the nightstand, my fingers fumbling until I find the bottle of sleeping pills. I don't open it. I just hold it, tightly.

Who is he?

The question circles my brain like a vulture.

Why can't I remember? Why does this faceless man feel like he was everything to me?

Tears slip down my cheeks before I even realize I'm crying. I draw the blanket around my shoulders and curl into myself, clutching the fabric like a child.

"It was just a dream," I whisper to myself.

I close my eyes again, letting the tears fall freely into the pillow.

FOURTEEN

SAVI

The kitchen is bathed in the soft golden light of early morning. The scent of freshly brewed coffee lingers in the air.

My husband, Eric, is seated in the breakfast nook when I step into the kitchen. He holds a steaming cup of coffee in one hand, in the other, his phone, as he scrolls through the morning news and emails from overnight. His dark hair is tousled, jaw scruffy, and he's wearing a soft gray T-shirt that stretches across his broad shoulders. Eric is the most handsome man I've ever seen in my life.

He always has been.

And he always will be.

When he sees me, he smiles.

"Good morning, my love." I cross the kitchen and press a kiss to the top of his head, inhaling the scent of him before pulling away.

Eric surprised me last night with an early arrival. Very early—two in the morning, in fact. I hadn't expected him home for a few more days. We embraced. Cuddled. Talked until almost three in the morning about my trip to New York, the craziness of it all, and how I thought of him a million times while I was there.

I feel his eyes on me as I tighten the belt on my flannel robe and walk to the coffee pot.

"You're up too early," he says.

I nod, glancing outside at the woods that surround our house, barely touched by dawn. Fog hovers just above the grass.

It's a cold, damp autumn morning.

"I wanted to spend time with you before you go into the office."

As (bad) luck would have it, we live close to the regional office of the trucking company where Eric works. They keep a cubicle for him to complete reports and train new hires when he's in town.

"Is Katie still asleep?" he asks.

"For another ten minutes, probably."

Katie is the type who can roll out of bed and be out the door—looking like a fashion model—in thirty minutes flat.

After heating up a pair of Katie's latest (and greatest) blueberry muffins and filling my coffee, I settle in across from my husband.

"How did you sleep?"

"Like a rock."

Eric takes half the muffin in one bite.

I love to watch him eat.

I love to watch him, period.

"I made a chiropractor appointment for you at four this afternoon."

He swallows, tilts his head, his eyes softening in adoration. "I don't know what I'd do without you."

"You'd drive trucks 365 days a year, and your spine would be twisted into a pretzel."

"Speaking of taking care of our bodies..." He reaches for the weekly pill planner on the counter and sets it in front of me. "Don't forget your morning pills, sweetheart."

"Oh, don't worry." I pop open the 'Thursday' tab and tap out the contents. "Katie is like the Gestapo with my pills—ever since you gave her that task." I roll my eyes.

"You always forget to take them," Eric responds, matter-of-factly. "And then you end up with an awful migraine. And the vitamins and supplements are important for your—*our*—health."

"Says the guy who sits for twenty hours a day."

He grins. "Fair point."

"When do you leave again?" I ask, stomach twisting at the thought.

"Tomorrow. I'm filling in for someone else."

I look down.

Just then, Katie stumbles into the kitchen, half asleep, hair in knots, night shirt twisted. She startles when she sees me, then her eyes shift across the table where Eric is sitting, then back to me.

"Oh—oh. I'm sorry... I didn't realize Eric was here—I didn't mean to interrupt."

"You're not interrupting," I say.

Katie smiles, but it doesn't quite reach her eyes. I wonder if she had a bad dream last night too. Her focus flickers again across the table.

"Well, I'll leave you two lovebirds alone." She smiles again, but seems nervous suddenly. Which is strange. Before I can ask what's wrong, Katie spins on her heel and disappears down the hallway.

Eric gets up, rounds the table, and pulls out the chair next to me.

"Hey." He gently lifts my chin and watches me with that quiet, knowing gaze of his. "You okay?"

"Yes." I force a smile. "I don't want you to leave tomorrow. I just miss you, is all."

"I know, and *you* know that..." Eric leans in, inches from my face, and taps my heart. "I am always—*always*—right here. Even when I'm not with you in physical form, I am always," he taps my heart again, "right here."

"I know."

And I do. Because he reminds me every single day.

Eric pulls me in for a long, deep kiss, making everything bad disappear.

After a moment, he pulls back, still holding my hands. "What's on your mind?"

I exhale softly, tracing my finger along the back of his hand. "I don't know what's wrong with me," I murmur.

"That's an interesting way to start a conversation."

I huff a small laugh, shaking my head. "I mean… I should be happy about everything that's happening. Happy that my dream of being a bestselling author came true. But…" I pause, glancing at him, hesitant. "I've been feeling more anxiety than usual lately. Like… like, really, *really* bad anxiety."

"Of course you feel that way," he says, his voice warm, solid. "You've never been in this position before. You spent years writing quietly in your little corner of the world, and now, suddenly, everyone's watching. That's a lot. It would be a lot for anyone."

I look down at our joined hands. "I feel like I should be enjoying it more. Like maybe I'm being ungrateful."

"You're not ungrateful," Eric says firmly. "You're human."

Tears fill my eyes. "Thank you. I needed to hear that."

He squeezes my hands. "Get out this morning. Go for a walk, a jog. Reconnect. Clear your head."

"You're always right."

"And don't you have an appointment with your therapist soon?"

I blink. "Oh. Yeah. Later this morning actually—I think. Thanks for the reminder."

Eric lifts my hand to his lips, pressing a gentle kiss to my knuckles. "Just remember, you're never alone in any of this. Okay?" He lifts his finger and gently taps my heart once more. "I'm always —*always*—right here."

I want to throw my arms around him. I want to cry and tell him how much I love him. How grateful I am. How I don't deserve him. How I don't want to let him down.

After all, I've let my husband down enough for two lifetimes.

FIFTEEN

JACOB

As I step out of the shower, my cell phone rings.

Grabbing a towel, I answer.

"Lockhart."

"Hey, Detective, it's Woodson. Did I wake you?"

"No."

Sergeant Andrew Woodson is a six-foot-three former line-backer with two kids and three ex-wives. A career cop, dedicated to the job above all else.

"Good. We got a call about a body," he continues. "Found in a cabin off Halsey Trail. Close to the encampment. Shultz and I responded." He pauses, voice shifting. "Looks like we're going to need you."

"Homicide?"

"Appears that way. Vic's been dead probably four or five days by the look of it. I've got Shultz blocking off the area now."

"Good. Don't let anyone else in until I get there. Give me fifteen."

"Got it. I'll send you the address and drop you a pin of the location. It's on the north end side of the trail. And Lockhart?"

"Yeah?"

"You might want to wait to eat breakfast."

. . .

The driveway is little more than a path—two narrow dirt ruts carved into the forest floor, swallowed on either side by thick underbrush and towering trees.

It's a cold, misty morning. Thick cloud cover blocks the rising sun, giving the forest an eerie blue glow. Fog sways just above the ground. Mother Nature did a fantastic job of setting the scene this morning.

I park behind Shultz's service vehicle, at the top of the driveway, pleased that the first responders knew not to drive up to the house and risk destroying tracks or trace evidence that may be lingering in the damp earth.

Pocketing my keys, I step out, slip on my leather jacket and backpack. Inside are multiple evidence collection kits, measuring devices, a notebook, gloves, booties, crime scene tape, luminal spray, a bottle of water, a can of antacids. I set off, my boots crunching over dead pine needles and patches of wet leaves.

My breath fogs as I step past the first strip of yellow crime scene tape strung between two saplings. It flutters weakly in the breeze, barely holding its own against the mist and gloom.

The cabin comes into view like a ghost, emerging from the fog as I approach. Even in daylight—what little of it filters through the dense gray clouds overhead—the place feels like something out of a horror film. A ruin of wood and moss and slow decay. The roof is sagging inward. The chimney's cracked down the middle. The window, barely a slit in the wall, is covered with a mildewed sheet that stirs in the wind.

Officer Woodson stands off to the right of the tiny yard, near a plastic bucket that, based on the amount of flies buzzing round it, is a makeshift toilet. He's questioning a man in a stained hoodie who rocks back and forth on his heels, arms crossed tightly over his chest. Judging by the man's slurred speech and glassy eyes, he's not offering much.

I assume the man is from the nearby encampment. In the

valley, about a hundred yards away, the pristine woods morph into a small encampment of tattered tents, rusting grocery carts, and makeshift shelters pieced together from discarded pallets.

The city has tried for years to rehabilitate the area—tried, and failed. Because homelessness isn't a crime. Because temporary solutions cost too much. Because no one can agree on what to do.

So the endless cycle continues.

A broken porch step groans under my weight as I climb it.

The door is open.

Camera flashes pop inside the one-room cabin, casting fleeting shadows along the walls. Jammie, the crime scene photographer, is crouched in the corner, holding a handkerchief over her nose with one hand, camera in the other. Next to her, the victim lies on a mattress on the floor. A cloud of flies buzz against a backdrop of dried blood streaking down the cracked wall.

Woodson was right.

I'm glad I skipped breakfast.

SIXTEEN

SAVI

After Eric and I say our goodbyes, I decide to knock out my once-weekly grocery shopping while it's still early in the morning.

Gripping the steering wheel with one hand, I use the other to fumble blindly in my purse until I finally find the vibrating cell phone buried at the bottom. Katie's name flashes on the screen.

I press the phone to my ear. "Hello?"

"Hey, babe—are you driving?" There's the slight tremor of nerves behind her voice.

"Yes. I'm heading to the grocery store before the crowds hit. What's going on? Aren't you at work?"

"I *was* at work."

"Oh no. What happened?"

"I got fired."

"*What?*"

"Yep. Not ten minutes after I walked into the clinic, my boss pulled me into his office and asked me to gather my things."

The casual way she says it, like she's commenting on the weather, makes my heart break. My best friend is a master at disso-ciating.

Katie recently accepted a position as a hospital case worker. We were both hopeful it would work out because the only other thing Katie is more passionate about than red blends is helping others.

"Katie—are you serious? You've only been working there a few months. What happened?"

"There's a ninety-day evaluation period. Apparently, I have made many, *many* mistakes during this period—like logging patient notes under the wrong patient... twice."

"Oh, hell." I exhale slowly, then I freeze, my brows drawing together. How odd—I literally *just* wrote about my fictional character, Lillian, getting fired.

What a strange coincidence.

"I'm so sorry," I say.

"Thanks. My boss was really flirty with me anyway, and I made sure he knew that I wasn't interested, and I think that pissed him off."

"Want me to slit his tires?"

"Done. Just joking."

"Okay, for real, what do you need from me right now? A dozen donuts? A massive hug?"

"I need it all," she exhales dramatically. "No, I'm going to treat myself to a nice, big breakfast and an eight-dollar coffee. Then I'm going to sit outside the café, watching the tourists come and go while wallowing in my misery. Then I might swing by and see my cousin who just had a baby. I've been putting it off."

"And then?"

"Then, I'll come home and hang out with my best friend. Did Eric leave?"

"Yes."

"I'm sorry, babe."

"It's okay."

Though I already miss Eric, I feel worse for Katie. Her track record with jobs isn't great. She either leaves after only a short time, or gets laid off, and she's getting to the age where second chances don't come as easily.

"Katie, it's going to be okay. Seriously, you've got everything you need at the house. We've got food, a roof over our heads. We're going to be just fine."

A pause. Then, softer, "Thanks, girl. Love you."

"Love you too."

After we disconnect, I toss the phone into my purse and turn left into Miller's Market, the only grocery store in town. It's nothing fancy—wood-paneled walls, a handful of aisles, an old neon *OPEN* sign buzzing faintly in the window, and that permanent smell of fresh produce and waxed linoleum.

I grab a cart from the entrance, the front wheel wobbling slightly, and let out a breath. Katie's call has only added to the foul mood I'm in, and now, I feel the slight throbbing of a headache forming behind my temples.

I take a deep breath and remind myself it's just another routine task. Bread, milk, coffee, something frozen so we don't have to think too hard about dinner later. In and out. Simple.

Except the moment I step inside, a random man greets me.

"Miss Portman," he says with a warm smile. "Good to see you."

I don't know this man.

"Thank you," I say, thinking: Great. Strangers are already beginning to recognize me from my newfound fame. But then he says—

"How are you feeling today?"

How am I feeling?

"Fine... thank you."

As I walk past, I glance over my shoulder. He's still standing there, still watching me with that same pleasant expression frozen on his face.

The store is quiet, just a handful of locals meandering through the aisles. The overhead fluorescents hum softly, one bulb near the dairy section flickering like it's struggling to stay alive.

I pause at the flower section and grab a dozen roses for Katie. Because flowers make everything better.

The wheel squeaks as I round to the next aisle.

I grab a can of soup—tomato, my favorite—but my fingers slip, and it tumbles toward the floor. Before it can even hit the ground, a woman, twice my age, swoops in, catching it effortlessly.

"Got it," she says, beaming as she hands it back to me.

I hesitate before taking it. "Thanks."

"Of course!" The woman lingers a second too long, eyes searching mine like she's looking for something. Finally, she nods and walks away, humming to herself. But when I glance over my shoulder, she's watching me from behind the endcap. And not in a you're-famous kind of way, but in a concerned kind of way.

Huh.

At the bread aisle, I reach for a loaf of sourdough, but the older man next to me gently nudges a different one toward me.

"This one's fresher," he says, smiling.

I thank him, take the one he suggested and move on.

Near the checkout, an elderly woman in a lavender coat brushes past me, shaking her head, and mutters just loud enough for me to hear, "Poor, poor thing."

My cart bumps into the display of granola bars, boxes toppling with a thud.

What? *Poor thing?* What did she mean by that?

Unable to let it go, I turn toward her. "Excuse me?"

But the woman doesn't look back. She continues down the aisle like she never said a word.

I stand there for a few seconds, trying to make sense of it. There is no one else in the aisle. The woman was clearly speaking to me—about me?

Poor thing.

My pulse starts to increase.

What is going on? Why is everyone acting so strangely?

Suddenly, the buzzing overhead lights seem louder, the air feels too still, and I want nothing more than to get out of here.

By the time I reach the register, I can barely remember what I came in for.

The cashier, a girl in her early twenties with wide, eager eyes, greets me like an old friend. "Hi, Miss Portman! Did you find everything okay?"

Miss Portman. Again.

"Uh, yeah. Just the usual."

As she scans my items, she suddenly frowns and holds up the loaf of bread. "Oh, wait, I think this might be on sale. Let me check for you!"

Before I can protest, the cashier darts away, disappearing into the aisles.

I glance at the people in line behind me. No one looks impatient. No one sighs or checks their watch. They're just... watching.

The girl returns moments later, breathless. "Yep! Fifty cents off!" She grins like she just delivered the most exciting news of my life.

"Oh," I clear my throat. "Lucky me. Thank you."

I pay, take my bag with a mumbled thanks, and all but bolt for the door.

As I walk toward my van, I notice the man who held the door for me earlier. He's still there, leaning casually against his truck, pretending to look at his phone.

But he's not. He's watching me under his lashes.

A slow, prickling sensation creeps up the back of my neck.

I climb into my inconspicuous powder-blue minivan and lock the doors.

Just then my phone rings. It's my therapist calling to remind me of our appointment in an hour.

Perfect timing.

SEVENTEEN
JACOB

The male victim is small in stature, sprawled on his back on the mattress, arms and legs splayed as if he died making a snow angel. A pool of blood has soaked through the vomit surrounding his head. His greasy black hair is plastered to a pale, gaunt face. Blue lips. Slack jaw, frozen mid-moan.

The man's black trench coat is flapped open, revealing a shredded T-shirt, drenched in dried blood.

The stench is horrific.

Shultz, the officer who responded with Woodson, is crouched in front of the body, next to Jammie who is taking her final pictures of the scene.

Officer Shultz is in his early twenties, the embodiment of youthful determination mixed with a professionalism that belies his age. He reminds me of myself, before the weight of the job took over.

He looks up as I step deeper into the cabin, swatting away the flies.

"Is that Rat?" I ask.

"Yep. Dewey 'Rat' Morrison." Shultz confirms. "Not the official ID, but yeah. I recognize him, too."

Jammie glances over her shoulder. "I don't recognize him; should I?"

"Everyone in Bear's Creek knows this man," Shultz explains. "Dubbed Rat, due to his unfortunate resemblance to the rodent, Dewey is a life-long drifter, a staple of the streets. After spending time in jail, he was released back into society where he quickly resorted back to drugs and alcohol to dull a troubled life. He'd been living here."

"Ah, that's right." She nods thoughtfully. "I remember now. He's the guy who the kids from that church—can't remember the name—have taken in, so to speak. They minister to him and ensure his basic human needs are met."

Shultz adds, "It's sparked its share of controversy. Are they helping him or enabling him? Are they fixing a problem or making it worse? The town is split down the middle—as it always will be."

"You and Woodson made the right call, calling me," I say, returning the attention to the body. "There's no way in hell this was an accidental death. Not with those wounds. Did you find the knife?"

Shultz stands, nodding at Jammie as she exits the cabin. "Nope. We searched inside and outside, but no luck finding the murder weapon. We'll search again once these damn clouds drift away."

"You call the coroner?" I ask.

Shultz nods. "Should be here any second."

"Let me get my time with the body first."

"As always."

I take in the scene.

A single bare bulb dangles from the ceiling, but it's long dead. The only illumination comes from the weak morning light sneaking past the fabric that covers the single window. Dust floats in the beams like slow-moving snow.

The room is sparse—no real furniture to speak of. Just a stained mattress in the corner, a dirty cooler next to it, its lid cracked open. Inside are a few cans of soup, a pack of bologna floating in a puddle of melted ice, and a half-drunk bottle of vodka. The floor is littered with trash, a stack of mismatched plastic containers, a few rolls of toilet paper, and a bible.

There's no sign of electricity. No running water. No sink. Just survival and decay.

There are also no signs of a struggle. Nothing knocked over. No blood trail suggesting the victim moved far. Whoever did this, did it fast. Either that or Rat never had a chance to fight back.

I tilt my head, examining the gaping wounds. "Who called it in?"

Shultz nods toward the window. Outside, just past a gnarled tree, Officer Woodson is still speaking with the same shaky, haggard-looking man I noticed as I approached the scene.

"That's the guy who called it in. Name's Charles. Says he came to check on Rat, after he hadn't seen him in a few days. Found him like this."

"What was he checking on him for?"

"The smell, and also, Rat promised him a pint of whiskey in exchange for a joint."

I take in Charles's unsteady stance, glassy eyes. The man can barely stand upright.

"He lives in the encampment down in the valley," Shultz continues.

"We'll want pictures of his shoes and the tread on the bottom. See which tracks outside are his and which are not."

Shultz grunts. "Yeah, he probably walked all over the crime scene, destroying evidence. For what it's worth, I don't think he did it. Why call it in?"

I nod.

"What else do you need?" he asks.

"I want everyone in the encampment interviewed. Somebody had to have seen or heard something. If they're passed out, wake them up. Get Loni to bring coffee for them, snacks. An incentive to wake up and speak."

"Good call." Shultz glances out the opened door. "We need to rope off the hiking trails. Tourists are already on morning hikes. They can see the top of the driveway from the trail, and they'll see the crime scene tape."

"The media will be here soon, too, if I had to guess. Keep them back."

"On it. Got an initial read on the scene?"

"It's emotional."

"I thought so, too," Schultz agrees thoughtfully. "This guy was dead well before the killer stopped stabbing. Whoever did this was angry."

"Agreed. We'll start with speaking with the folks at Highpoint Church. The kids who looked after him. Then we'll pull street cams—the regular intersections where he hangs out. See if he has any repeat visitors."

"We need to consider the drug angle, too. You saw all the burned spoons and pipes?"

I nod. "We'll see what his toxicology says."

A distant echo of voices across the valley pull our attention. The encampment is waking up.

"Get this place secured," I say. "That's the priority right now."

As Shultz steps outside, I grab a handkerchief from my pocket, put it over my nose, and crouch next to the body.

A gust of wind whips the fabric curtain in the window above me.

The first thing I notice is that the assailant didn't slit the decedent's throat, which would have allowed for a much faster death. Again, this suggests a personal, emotional attack.

An earring twinkles from Rat's ear. My gaze shifts to the tarnished, cracked watch on his wrist, then to the half-empty bag of sliced bread in the corner. Not a robbery gone bad.

I then lean closer and study his fingernails. They are long, yellowed, and caked with dirt. However, they do not appear to be torn and there are no marks on his hands. This suggests he didn't fight his assailant. Not particularly surprising considering the puddle of vomit under his head. He was likely heavily under the influence.

Did he know his assailant? Or was he simply too high to respond?

After slipping on a pair of gloves, I reach into Rat's pockets. Aside from an old candy wrapper, empty.

Adjusting the handkerchief over my nose, my focus settles on the thick, gaping stab wounds speckling the man's torso. I wonder about the murder weapon.

A hunting knife? Carving knife? Kitchen knife?

My gaze sweeps the floor and I take note of the faded muddy tracks around the body. There was heavy rain about five days ago, which would have made the ground outside prime for prints. Deciding that this will be my first focus, I retrieve my phone and begin taking my own photos. I'll need to take a cast of each dried print in the yard, then venture outside the property and check the trails.

As I stare down at the most visible dried boot print, picturing a muddy shoe, a tingle of unease slithers up my spine. A distant, yet unformed memory tapping at my subconscious.

A whisper of warning.

EIGHTEEN
SAVI

Dr. Lin's clinic is quiet this morning. Calmer than usual. Probably because I'm her first client of the day.

Inside her office, the diffuser on her bookshelf fills the room with a soft scent of lavender. Muted sunlight slants through the tall windows in hazy ribbons, catching on the glass picture frames and polished stones that line her desk.

She sits across from me in her usual soft gray cardigan and sensible heels, her notebook resting in her lap, pen poised like always.

I sit stiffly on the couch, arms folded across my chest, like always.

"I had another dream last night," I say, before she can even ask.

Her brow lifts just slightly. "The same one?"

I nod, chewing on my thumbnail for a second before forcing my hand back into my lap. "Yes."

I don't need to recap that the dream I'm referring to is the faceless man who dies of a heart attack. She's heard it plenty of times before.

Dr. Lin is quiet for a moment, then, "Did you see his face this time?"

I shake my head. "No. But somehow I love him—even though I

don't know who he is. In that bone-deep, soul-level kind of way. Like my heart is wired to his."

Dr. Lin nods and scribbles something into her notebook. "And how did you feel when you woke up?"

I look down at my lap, at my fingers interlaced on my lap so tightly my knuckles are white. "I was devastated. I cried. And then, weirdly, I began thinking about Katie."

She watches me for a beat longer than necessary. Then she flips a page in her notebook.

"Savi, we've talked before about how the mind sometimes stores memories in fragments. Dreams like these can sometimes be echoes of buried memories that perhaps you've forgotten. Not literal truths, but emotional ones."

I nod like I understand, though I'm not sure I do. I've never watched a man die of a heart attack before. Of that, I am certain.

I shift uncomfortably in my seat, brushing a piece of lint from my jeans just to give my hands something to do. She must notice, because her tone softens even more.

"What did it feel like in the dream?" she asks. "Not just emotionally—but physically. Were you running? Frozen? Trapped?"

The word hits me in the chest like a baseball bat.

"Trapped—*yes!* It's funny you used that word. That's exactly how it felt. I couldn't move. Couldn't breathe. I knew something terrible was about to happen, but I was stuck. Like, literally stuck. I couldn't help him."

Dr. Lin nods. "That's something we've touched on before. Your feelings of being trapped—emotionally or physically. It appears to be a major trigger for dreams and migraines."

I begin chewing on my lip, feeling a rush of emotion I can't explain.

Why do I feel like I'm about to cry?

"What's making you feel like you're trapped right now?

When I don't answer, she presses.

"Do you feel trapped in your career right now?" she asks, reading my mind.

"Yes," I blurt. "Oh my God, *yes*. The contract I signed. The book tour they're planning. The interviews. The deadlines. The pressure to be someone I'm not—or don't feel like I am, anyway. Honestly? I feel like I'm living someone else's life. And the thing is, I feel so *guilty* for feeling this way. Like I'm ungrateful."

"It's a lot of pressure," she says gently, then, "pressure you don't have to have, Savi. Tell me this: why do you feel trapped?"

"Because of their expectations, I guess."

"Are you responsible for other people's expectations?"

"No."

"Do you have a choice in your career?"

"No—yes... yes, I guess I do. I can always walk away."

Dr. Lin smiles. "So then, in the literal sense, you are not trapped in your career. You have choices, and you are never, ever responsible for others' expectations of you. That's on them, not you. Let me ask you this. Do you want to walk away from it all? Because now we have just established that option is available to you. You can get out, so to speak."

I hesitate. "No, I don't. This has been my dream for a long time." I snort. "Which is ironic considering my *actual* dreams lately."

Dr. Lin nods again, scribbles something down. "Let's try a grounding technique."

I swallow deeply as she sets her notebook aside.

"One we haven't used before," she continues. "It's something I've found helpful with clients who feel disconnected from themselves, especially during moments of intense emotion."

"Like dreaming of a faceless man dying?"

Her mouth tilts into a small smile. "Exactly."

She walks me through a method called 5-4-3-2-1, naming things I can see, hear, feel, smell, and taste. At first, it feels silly. Mechanical. Like some exercise from a first-grade mindfulness workbook.

But halfway through, something inside settles.

As we finish, Dr. Lin leans forward slightly, her tone still light but purposeful. "Let's keep an eye on how much this particular dream is resurfacing lately. And if you're willing, next time we can try a method called image re-scripting. It's a gentle way of rewriting recurring dreams—letting your subconscious take control of the narrative."

As I leave the office and step out into the bleak autumn morning, instead of feeling better, like I usually do, I feel worse. A weird, nervous energy.

An instinct that something is coming.

NINETEEN

TBD – A Thriller

Inspired by the mysterious Quinn and Jacob Lockhart of Bear's Creek.

Written by: Savanna Portman

Lillian

I am *pregnant.*

The two little (very unexpected) blue lines send an explosion of emotions through me.

I. Am. *Pregnant!*

Could this be the catalyst that will turn everything around? The thing that will pull me from the bottle, from the self-loathing, from the depths of whatever depressive hole I've been living in? Will it give me a sense of purpose? A way to make our marriage strong again.

I snatch my phone off the nightstand. I need to tell Andrew. He's going to be so excited—

Wait.

Will he be excited?

I'm not sure this is what Andrew wants to hear right now. After all, he couldn't even look at me the other night when I presented myself naked on a metaphorical silver platter for him.

I stare at my reflection in the mirror, my heart beginning to pound with doubt. My gaze drops to my bloated midsection.

I realize now, it's been growing for weeks. I thought it was the wine.

How is this happening so fast?

My breathing shallows.

I'm about to get fat. Oh, God, I'm going to get *fat.*

A crushing panic squeezes the air from my lungs. Andrew is not sexually attracted to me *as is.* How much worse will it be when I'm fat?

My thoughts begin to race.

Stretch marks. Swollen ankles. Acne. Puffy face. Andrew looking at me with disgust. Andrew never touching me again.

Instead of being the catalyst to turn our marriage around, could this be the thing that makes him finally leave me?

No. That can't happen.

I spin around, rip open my closet, and pull on a sports bra, tank, leggings, shoes.

I yank my ponytail so tight my scalp stings. I brush my teeth until my gums bleed.

After grabbing a jogging jacket, I step outside. The Lockhart Estate was built on a flat patch of land halfway up Plummet Heights, the tallest mountain in the area. One of my favorite things about the location is that I can pick up the hiking trails about two hundred meters from our backyard.

The second I step out of the back gate and into the woods that surround the property, my phone alerts me.

I stop, open the text from Andrew.

> Have a good jog. Do *not* turn off your track location.

I stare at the phone.

I'm pregnant, I want to respond. But I don't. I need to come to terms with this (massive) pivotal moment in my life before telling him. So, instead, I type—

Thanks. Yes, I know.

I glance over my shoulder at the security cameras where he is watching.

Always watching.

After securing my phone in the side-pocket of my leggings, I begin on the footpath through the woods that leads to the main hiking trail. The mid-morning sun dapples the forest floor in shimmering gold dots. The air is perfumed with the scent of fallen pine needles.

It's a beautiful morning, but I am acutely aware of my stomach. I place my hand there several times, as if needing to remind myself that it's true. That I have a baby growing in there.

That I will be better for it. That I will *not* gain weight, and that I will control this.

Pushing into a jog, I recall the last time Andrew and I had sex, around nine weeks ago. He was drunk, the only way he'll ever have sex with me. It was cold, mechanic, and sloppy. Loveless.

And now I'm pregnant.

I run harder.

Quickly, I begin to feel lightheaded and queasy. My legs suddenly feel like elephant trunks, my body like I'm moving through water.

Push through, Lillian. Be better.

The feeling intensifies with a piercing headache.

I remember then that not only did I forget to eat breakfast, but I vomited several times as well. My blood sugar is crashing.

I feel very, very sick.

My vision blurs and little black dots appear.

I reach out for the tree trunk next to me, but my knees buckle a split second before everything turns to black.

TWENTY
SAVI

With tears streaming down my cheeks, I close the laptop and push away from the desk. Lillian, my fictional character, is pregnant. Because of course she is. I am torturing myself with this manuscript and I don't know why.

Wiping my cheeks, I walk to the window and stare into the foggy, gray morning.

I try the 5-4-3-2-1 method my therapist suggested to "ground" me. But it doesn't work.

For years Eric and I tried for a baby. Years of hoping. Of Eric holding me every time my period came, whispering, *It's okay. I still love you. It'll happen when it's supposed to.*

Years of letting my husband down.

Years of failing at the one thing I was built to do.

After washing the mess off my face, I pull on my jogging clothes, just like Eric suggested I do this morning before he left, and just like my character Lillian did. Except unlike her, I'm not pregnant. While Lillian is jogging to stay fit for her pregnancy, I am jogging to punish my body for failing to get pregnant.

A low simmer of anger pulses through me as I drive through town, to the trails.

Writing about Lillian's pregnancy has cracked something open in me.

I had written it in a trance. My fingers had flown over the keyboard, filling the page with her reaction. The shock. The panic. The pure, raw terror at gaining weight.

And when I read it back, I realized just how fucked up it all is.

How *unfair* it is.

My fictional character has what I want—and she is afraid of it. Meanwhile, I'd give anything to be in her position.

Just as the tears begin to well in my eyes, the gas light turns on, reminding me that my powder-blue minivan is as empty as I am.

TWENTY-ONE
SAVI

A lone truck idles at the farthest pump, its exhaust curling into the cool autumn air. Beyond it, gray skies hang over the dense forest that surrounds the gas station. The whole morning feels shrouded in misery.

The place itself is classic Bear's Creek—faded signage, a crooked canopy that rattles when the wind gusts just right, and a cracked parking lot patched with years of half-hearted repairs. An "OPEN" sign buzzes faintly next to a hand-painted sign that reads: *Walton's Fuel & Feed*. It's the kind of place that sells motor oil, bait worms, and cheap coffee in equal measure.

I park at the nearest pump, step out, and swipe my card. The smell of gasoline hangs thick in the air. I yank my beanie lower over my ears, shivering. As the tank fills, I stare into the forest behind the station. It looks creepy. Like the kind of place where people disappear. And for the first time since leaving the house, I second-guess my morning jog.

But that's ridiculous.

The pump clicks off, startling me. I replace the nozzle and decide to grab a bottle of water. The bell above the door rings when I step inside.

A wall of thick, warm humid air swallows me whole. It smells like old grease, microwave burritos, and cheap air freshener. A freezer hums in the back, and overhead, a small radio crackles through the speakers, playing an '80s power ballad.

The cashier is an elderly Asian man with wire-rimmed glasses and a gray newsboy cap. He greets me with a warm nod.

I offer a polite smile and move toward the cooler. But before I can even reach for a bottle—

"Hey," he calls out.

I pause, hand hovering over the glass door. "Yes?"

His thin lips twitch into a grin. "Hey, you."

Oh no, here we go. He probably wants an autograph.

"You owe me five bucks," he says.

My fingers slip off the door handle. I turn fully toward him, my brow furrowing. "I'm sorry—what?"

The man laughs, shaking his head like I'm trying to pull a fast one on him. "Oh no, ma'am, you're not getting away that easily."

I force a polite smile. "I think you've got me confused with someone else."

"Nope." His grin widens. "I never forget a face. You were in here four or five nights ago, late. Around midnight. Bought a pack of cinnamon gum and winter gloves I had on sale. Trust me, I never forget a face."

"No, I—"

"Yep," he interrupts. "A replay of the football game was on, and you bet me five dollars that my team would lose. They didn't." He winks and extends his hand. "Pay up."

For a moment, I just stare at him.

I didn't come here four or five nights ago—and especially not at midnight. I didn't bet this man anything. I didn't buy cinnamon gum or gloves.

A strange, tight feeling curls through my stomach.

I could argue, but now all I want to do is get out of here. So instead, I let out a small laugh, playing along, even though my hands have gone clammy. "Okay, fine, let me just grab my water first."

I snatch the first bottle I see.

As I walk back to the register, I feel his eyes on me. I quickly place the bottle on the counter, dig into my wallet and slide a five-dollar bill across the counter. He slides it right back.

"Keep it," he says, smiling. "You don't have to pay up. I was just joking."

"Thanks," I mutter, paying for the water.

"Never bet against me," he says, wagging a finger. "My team always wins."

"Okay, yes." I force another smile. "Lesson learned."

But as I grab my bottle and turn for the door, the man grabs my wrist.

I freeze, look down at his fingers. Then up at his face.

His grin is gone.

"You take care of yourself, okay?" he says, voice lower. "And be careful out there."

I swallow. "Okay."

When he releases me, I spin on my heel and don't look back.

The wind hits me like a slap as I hurry out of the station. I get into my van, lock the doors, and sit there for a second, gripping the steering wheel, my pulse hammering in my ears.

Just to be sure, I pop open the center console. No cinnamon gum. No gloves.

I check the back seat. The side pockets. The glove compartment.

Nothing.

I snort, shaking my head. This is ridiculous.

The guy was wrong.

He mistook me for someone else. A simple mistake.

Nothing more.

TWENTY-TWO

JACOB

A flurry of voices rise in the distance, growing louder by the minute.

The media is here.

"Damn vultures," I mutter, squinting through the trees at the camera crew setting up at the top of the driveway. A familiar figure stands at the front of the pack—Andi Blake. Young, blonde, relentless. Always the first reporter on the scene, always the last to leave. I'd admire her hustle if I didn't loathe the media.

Behind her, a crowd is growing. Both tourists and local hikers, who ventured off the trail to see what the commotion was about.

In a town like Bear's Creek, keeping a crime scene quiet is damn near impossible—especially when there's a dead body involved. News and gossip spread faster than wildfire.

My gaze flicks over to Shultz and Woodson, making sure they've got the situation under control.

I turn away from the spectacle and kneel on the cold dirt, focusing on the dried boot print in front of me. Lifting my magnifying glass, I study the deep impression, left behind in the damp earth.

Something about it feels wrong.

I set down my pack and retrieve my tape measure. The wind whistles through the trees, muffling growing noise from the crowd.

The other prints around the cabin were easy to categorize. Most of them belong to Rat himself, judging by the size and worn-down boot tread. Another set, leading to and from the front door, presumably belongs to Charles—the man who found him.

But this one doesn't match. The tread is different. Lighter. More distinct.

Running shoes.

"Jesus. Someone could have warned me about the smell."

I glance up to see Doctor Mack Dempsey gliding down the driveway. The wind must have carried the scent from the cabin. The county coroner is dressed in his typical uniform—khaki trench coat over a blue dress shirt, with a pair of square glasses perched slightly askew on his nose.

"What you got there?" he asks, peering at the patch of dirt I'm studying.

"Running shoe. I think." I reply, studying the pattern again. "Doesn't match the others. Not Rat's. Not the guy who found him."

"Think you can get a cast?"

"Yeah. Just taking measurements first. I can do that later, though. Come check out the body."

Together, we step inside the cabin. Mack secures a face mask and takes a long moment to study the body.

"Someone didn't like this guy very much." He kneels beside the mattress, slipping on latex gloves. He lifts one of Rat's arms. Bugs scatter like ants.

"No defensive wounds, at first look." Mack confirms my initial thoughts. "No signs of struggle, from what I can see. He was likely too out of it to resist." He tilts his head, inspecting the largest of the stab wounds. "This was definitely a blade. The cuts are too clean to suggest any other material like metal or wood, or any kind of tool."

"What's your guess on the size of the blade?"

"I'll need to confirm that during the autopsy, but visually? Four to six inches." He exhales through his nose. "But I will say this is a classic in-and-out stabbing. No dragging, no sawing. Just... precision."

The shower scene in *Psycho* flashes through my head.

This wasn't about vengeance. This was about pain. A different kind of rage. Again, everything about this suggests it was an emotional kill.

A rustling noise outside pulls my attention. I turn as Shultz steps into the cabin. He and Mack nod at each other in greeting.

"The crowd is getting restless," he informs us.

"Get the hikers out of here immediately—but make sure everyone from the nearby encampment stays. We need to question everyone. Someone here knows something. Is Loni here with the coffee and snacks yet?"

"She's on her way."

"Good. Whoever is asleep, wake them up. If they're passed out, sober them up. They all know Rat, and I want to know what they know."

"You got it, boss. What do you want me to tell Andi Blake?"

"To fuck herself."

"Verbatim?"

I grunt, return my focus to the body.

Shultz chuckles before stepping outside. He knows not to repeat that. He also knows I mean it.

As Mack gets to work, I step back to allow for space.

My gaze shifts to the faded muddy print next to the body. The one that matches the sneakers outside. It's smeared slightly at the toe, like the person pivoted abruptly—like they ran.

TWENTY-THREE
SAVI

I've chosen the north entry of the trail this morning. It's a lesser-known starting point, one that will force a longer, harder route around the mountain—exactly what I need. I want to push myself to exhaustion, let the miles clear my head and release this uneasy, anxious feeling that has settled in my bones.

I decide that I'll run up the mountain to the peak, take a few minutes to spy on the Lockhart Estate from the ridge, then loop back to my van.

I pull onto the grassy shoulder, frowning at the number of vehicles parked here. Tourists don't know this spot. Something is up.

Then, I notice that two of the vehicles are police cars, one unmarked.

Huh.

Shoving the van into park, I hesitate, glancing at the tree line. The police are probably here as part of their ongoing effort to patrol the growing encampment. That's probably all it is.

I cut the engine.

The morning air bites my cheeks, slipping through the gaps of my jacket as I stretch beside the van. After securing my beanie over my ears, I take off.

The first half-mile is brutal. As I ascend the second rolling hill, I see a flash of yellow in the distance.

I slow, squinting at the DO NOT CROSS tape stretched between two trees ahead. Beyond it, blurred figures shift through the trees, and voices carry on the wind.

I come to a stop, and a sudden wave of nausea slams into me. I close my eyes, bend forward, and brace my hands against my knees. Tiny black dots blur my vision.

Another damn headache.

Once the dizziness fades, I straighten, more worried about what is happening in the woods than my headache. I step off the trail, and pick my way to the crowd that has formed at the top of what appears to be someone's driveway.

At the bottom of the drive I see a dilapidated cabin and a small group of officers. A tall man is speaking to another man with salt and pepper hair and a leather jacket with collar flipped up against the wind.

It's Jacob Lockhart! The local homicide detective. The inspiration for the lead male character in my fictional novel. The owner of the home I obsessively watch. The husband to Quinn, whom I've never once seen in real life.

Just then, two men emerge from the trees behind me. One is an officer, the other a haggard-looking man wrapped in layers of ragged clothing. His bloodshot eyes are wide and wild beneath the shadow of his hood.

They see me.

I freeze.

The officer's gaze sharpens. "Ma'am, this area is roped off. I need you to immediately—"

"It's her!" the man yells frantically, pointing a finger directly at me.

I look behind me. There's no one else here.

The officer calls the man Charles as he stumbles forward, jabbing a gloved hand in my direction. "It's her! It's her! She's the one who was sneaking around Rat's cabin!"

My heart stops.

What? I don't understand. Who the hell is Rat?

The officer frowns, eyes narrowing as he studies me.

I take a step back. "I—I think you have me confused with—"

"Arrest her!" Charles's voice is shrill with panic. "It's her! She killed him! She killed Rat!"

The breath whooshes from my lungs.

The officer's hand twitches toward his belt. Toward his radio—or his gun?

I turn and I run.

"Get her!"

"Ma'am! Stop!"

I don't stop. Instead, I sprint. Harder than I ever have in my life.

My blood roars in my ears, drowning out their shouts behind me. My head pounds as I fly across the uneven terrain, dodging roots, hurdling rocks, blindly following the twisting path back to the trailhead.

I don't look back. Not until I'm in my van, my hands trembling so badly I can barely press the ignition.

The moment the engine roars to life, I peel out of the lot, tires spitting gravel behind me.

What *the hell* is happening?

TWENTY-FOUR
SAVI

The man's words echo on repeat in my head as I speed into the garage, nearly clipping the top of the van on the door before it opens fully.

"Arrest her! She killed him! She killed Rat!"

I stagger out of the van. My keys slip through my trembling hands, hitting the garage floor with a *clink*. I don't pick them up. All I want to do is get inside my house.

"Eric?" I call out hoarsely as I open the door, though I know he isn't here. But I say his name anyway, desperate for something familiar. Something safe.

The walls feel too close, too suffocating. Like they're trapping me.

I close my eyes.

Breathe, Savi. Just breathe.

Katie isn't home either. And a part of me is grateful because dealing with my spiraling drama is the last thing she needs after getting fired. She's already worried about me. I don't want her to see me like this.

I stumble to the kitchen and grip the counter. My reflection stares back at me in the window above the sink—wide-eyed, pale, wild.

What *the hell* is happening?

Who is Rat? And why did that man accuse me of killing him?

I turn on the faucet and splash cold water on my face. The shock of it barely registers. My hands fumble toward the cabinet where I keep my medication. I tap out two migraine painkillers and chase them with the first thing I see—an opened bottle of wine Katie left on the counter last night. The room-temperature liquid is bitter and acidic, sliding down my throat like bile.

I don't even know why I just did that. I don't need a drink. *I don't drink.*

I flatten my palms on the counter, bow my head, and take a deep breath.

Think, Savi. Think.

What do we know to be true? My therapist taught me this. In moments where I feel overwhelmed, I am supposed to stop and think: what is true in *this* moment?

Okay. First, the man at the gas station swore I was there in the middle of the night, sometime last week. He swore that I'd made a bet with him. Which is insane. I wasn't there, and I would never wager with a total stranger over a stupid football game. I don't even like football.

Second, thirty minutes later, a homeless man at a crime scene points to me—*me*—and claims I killed a man named Rat. The apparent victim of the crime scene I happened upon.

Thirdly, and perhaps most unsettling of all, just days ago, while drafting my thriller, I wrote a scene where my female lead character murdered *a man* in *a cabin*—in the *middle of the woods*.

What are the odds of that?

What are the odds of *any* of this?

I remind myself that I don't know the manner in which the man died. It could have been natural causes, or an overdose. Likely not a stabbing as I'd written about in my manuscript. My manuscript is not predicting the future. I am not some crazy clairvoyant. That is *insane*.

I squeeze shut my eyes, willing the thoughts away, but they only slam into me harder.

But what if they're right? What if I did go to the gas station last week? What if I was in those woods? What if I did kill someone?

A sickening possibility roots itself in my brain. It's absurd, ridiculous, but it latches on anyway: Sleepwalking. Isn't that a thing? And also sleep-driving?

What if I *did* go out? What if I was there and just don't remember?

I clutch the counter, forcing myself to stay grounded, forcing my thoughts into some kind of logical order.

No. No. I'm being ridiculous. I take prescription pills to help me sleep. Katie ensures that I do. Also, why *the hell* would I kill someone?

You are being crazy, Savi.

It's just a weird series of coincidences.

But it's *really* weird, right?

Before I can stop myself, I pull my phone from my jacket pocket, fingers fumbling as I scroll through my contacts.

The line rings once before it picks up.

"Hello?"

"Dr. Lin? It's Savi. I'm so sorry—I know we just met, but—" My voice cracks. "I need to ask you something. I'm curious if I've ever brought up sleepwalking before?"

A pause, then, "No. You've never mentioned sleepwalking before. Not once, actually. Is this something you're experiencing now?"

"I—I don't know." I press the heel of my palm into my temple, willing the pressure to relieve the drumming in my brain. "I don't know, I was just, uh, curious," I lie pitifully.

She's quiet for a beat.

"You're still taking the sleep aid I prescribed, correct?"

"Yes. Every night. Katie ensures I take it."

"Then it's highly unlikely you'd be sleepwalking, Savi. That medication is a sedative and would prevent that kind of motor activity. And again, you've never brought up anything like this before—not even in passing."

I feel relieved, and also *not* relieved at the same time.

"Savi," she says gently. "Can you tell me more about what happened to lead up to this call?"

"Nothing, really. I was just curious."

"Savi—"

"I'm okay," I lie. "Really. I'm just tired."

There's another pause. I can tell she doesn't believe me. Then, "Would you like to come back in this afternoon? I have an opening—"

"No, it's okay. I'm sorry I bothered—"

"Savi, I'm penciling you in right now. I want to see you this afternoon."

I exhale. "Okay. I guess I need it. Thanks."

"Savi," she catches me before I hang up. "Why don't you write until then?"

"Write?"

"Yes. Writing is your happy place. When the world feels like it's crumbling around you, you slip into your own little fictional world and disappear like magic. Keep your brain busy, get your thoughts out on paper—through your characters."

TWENTY-FIVE

SAVI

Heeding Dr. Lin's advice, I've settled in at my desk with a steaming cup of coffee.

Just write, Savi. Focus on your fictional story—what you can control.

The phone buzzes on the desk next to me. I glance at the screen. Vivienne.

I hesitate, cup hovering near my lips.

Answer it.

On a heavy sigh, I set down my mug and pick up the phone.

"Darling!" Viv's voice is a burst of energy, as always. I picture her in her Manhattan office, perched at her glass desk, a designer scarf around her neck, a vape pen in one hand, phone in the other. "How did it go? Was it everything we dreamed?"

The local bookstore signing. Right. It feels like so long ago.

"It was great," I say, keeping my voice light. "Big turnout. Lots of readers."

"Of course it was a big turnout! You're a star, Savi. And the local press was there, correct?"

I force a smile, even though she can't see it. "Yeah, they were great."

"Good, good! Now did you get my email about the morning show?"

I swallow deeply. "I did. Can I have a few more days to consider it?"

She pauses. "Well, yes, I suppose—but it's a *massive* opportunity, honey. Every author's dream. I'll need to know by the end of the week. Now. Tell me you've already finished the synopsis for the first book in the new contract?"

My stomach tightens.

The contract—that I *just* signed—consists of three more cozy mysteries, each with carefully crafted small-town charm, quirky characters, and a neatly wrapped-up ending.

"Yes." My fingers tighten around the phone. "I just need to shore up a few things before sending it off to Eliot."

"That's my girl! Stay on schedule, okay? We've got momentum, and I want to keep it rolling. The readers are waiting for the book, and so is Eliot."

"Of course," I murmur, already shifting my gaze to my laptop.

"Well, I won't keep you, darling," Viv chirps. "Get back to writing. I can't wait to see what you come up with!"

We hang up.

For a long moment, I stare at the blinking cursor on the screen. Then, I click not into the cozy mystery, but instead into my thriller, a fictional account of the mysterious Quinn and Jacob Lockhart.

The last chapter I wrote glares back at me.

I run harder, faster… I begin to feel lightheaded and queasy…. my vision blurs and little black dots appear…

I blink, staring at the scene that eerily mimics what *just* happened to me on the trail.

Chapter one begins with my lead character, Lillian, murdering a man in a cabin in the woods.

Later, she gets fired from volunteer work—just as Katie had gotten fired from her job.

Then, she goes for a jog on the trail and gets sick—just like I just did.

"No." I say firmly to myself. "Stop. Savi."

I won't allow myself to think too much into this. My manuscript is not predicting the future. Period.

On a deep inhale, my fingers hover over the keyboard

Just keep writing...

TWENTY-SIX

TBD – A Thriller

Inspired by the mysterious Quinn and Jacob Lockhart of Bear's Creek.

Written by: Savanna Portman

Lillian

The first thing that registers is the sharp scent of stale alcohol wafting over my face. Then, the sensation of pressure—strong, calloused hands braced against my ribcage. Then, a frantic voice...

"Hey! Lady! Come on now, wake up; don't do this to me—"

I jolt awake with a weak gasp, my arms flailing, instinctively swatting at the figure looming over me. My vision wobbles, but I catch a glimpse of wild eyes and an unkempt beard before the man jerks back with an exaggerated exhale.

"*Christ,* woman," the man grunts, falling back onto his haunches. "Scared the hell outta me."

I'm trembling. My skin is clammy and sweaty. The ground is damp and cold beneath me, and when I shift, pain flares up the back of my skull.

I touch the spot gingerly, wincing at the swollen bump.

"You dropped like a damn plank," the man says, wiping his palms down the front of his tattered jacket. "Passed out cold. Thought you were dead."

Dead?

My hand flies to my stomach. I'm not dead—the baby is okay.

I squeeze my eyes shut, trying to piece together the last few moments.

The jog. The lightheadedness. The sick feeling in my stomach, the black spots in my vision. Low blood sugar.

How could I have let this happen? I should have known better. I should have eaten before running. I am pregnant, after all. How could I be so careless?

Disappointment washes over me. My first real test of taking care of this baby, and I'd already failed.

I sit up, pulling my legs in toward my chest.

"You sick?" the man asks, studying me now, his gaze more observant than concerned.

I look him over. He's gaunt, dirt-streaked, and wrapped in a patchwork of coats and hoodies, all in varying states of disrepair. A knit beanie clings to his head, with greasy strands of gray hair curling at the edges. His eyes are surprisingly sharp, though.

I hesitate. This man is a complete stranger. But then again, he's the one who saved me.

"I'm not sick," I finally say, "I'm pregnant."

The word feels weird rolling off my lips.

"Huh. Okay, well…" He scratches at his chin, nodding. "I remember when my sister was pregnant. She passed out once. Maybe twice? Turns out she just needed to eat."

Smart man.

He reaches into his pocket and pulls out a crumpled package of peanut butter crackers. His hands are dirty, his nails blackened from life on the streets. He holds the packet out toward me.

"No, I—"

"Just eat 'em," he insists, shaking the pack. "I can't carry you back to wherever you came from. So, eat."

There's something oddly parental, and comforting, about his tone.

"What's your name?" I ask, regarding him closely.

"They call me Wally."

"Do they call you Wally because it's not your real name?"

A craggy grin spreads across his face, revealing a few missing teeth. "Bingo. Real name's Harvey."

"What's wrong with Harvey?"

His grin falters a bit. "Harvey's got a long history attached to it. One I'm not real proud of."

I nod slowly. "I get it."

"Doubt it." He shakes the crackers at me. "Take them. Eat. You're as pale as a ghost."

My hands are trembling so badly that Harvey has to tear open the package for me.

He watches closely as I shove two crackers into my mouth. They feel like sandpaper on my dry tongue, but I chew and swallow them down anyway.

When I try to hand the rest back, he shakes his head. "No, ma'am. Eat the whole damn thing."

"No, I can't. They're yours and—"

"Don't disrespect me—or that baby in your belly. I got more. Just eat."

I smile softly. "Thank you."

Harvey watches me eat the entire pack, and within just a few minutes, it's as if a switch flips. The dizziness fades, the headache eases. The difference is remarkable.

I exhale, leaning back on my hands. "Wow. That really worked."

Harvey smirks. "Told ya. Drink a big glass of orange juice as soon as you get home."

I'd rather drink a big glass of wine, I think.

He offers me a hand, and I take it. His grip is firm, but surprisingly gentle as he helps me to my feet.

"Thank you," I say, meaning it.

"Don't mention it."

I pause. "Hey, Wally? Don't tell anyone I'm pregnant."

"Don't tell anyone my real name's Harvey."

I grin. "Deal."

An hour later, I pull into a narrow parking spot on the edge of Main Street, still thinking about Wally. The way he helped me without hesitation. The way he hadn't judged me, hadn't asked for anything in return. He'd given me the only food he had on him.

I'm surprised, grateful, and incredibly humbled. So, I make a decision. I'm going to buy this stranger as many packs of peanut butter crackers as I can find, and deliver them personally.

The boutique grocery store on the corner has an entire shelf of them, ironically called Harv's Crackers. I almost laugh. If that's not a sign, I don't know what is. I empty the shelf and grab a dozen bottles of water.

With a full bag in my arms, I step back out onto the street. But instead of heading straight to my car, I pause outside Karen's Gifts, when the window display catches my eye.

Six crib mobiles hang from the ceiling—sun, moon, stars—over a baby-themed display. A fuzzy brown bunny sits in the center, floppy ears draped over its feet. Next to him, a matching octopus and a blue whale. But my eyes are locked on the cutest pair of fuzzy, purple leopard-print baby booties.

A strange, warm feeling spreads through me and for the first time, the reality of this hits me. I am going to be a mother. And it's a girl. Somehow, I just know it.

A small smile curves my lips as I step inside and buy my baby her very first gift—along with a big bottle of red I purchased while at the grocery store.

TWENTY-SEVEN

TBD - A Thriller

Inspired by the mysterious Quinn and Jacob Lockhart of Bear's Creek.

Written by: Savanna Portman

Lillian

Four months later...

I look like I'm having triplets.

I'm not.

None of my clothes fit. Not a single damn pair of pants.

My entire torso has widened, my face has rounded, and by the end of the day, my feet are so swollen I have to prop them up every night. Even my hands look different—fat. Everything about me is changing. Expanding. Taking up more space than I ever have in my life.

On top of it all, I'm three months sober.

Fine—false. I am *mostly* three months sober. The truth is, the first two months were hell. The craving was all-consuming. I snuck an occasional glass just to keep the withdrawal symptoms at bay. My husband, Andrew, doesn't know this, of course.

But eventually, I weaned myself off the booze, and now, I'm here—at the five-month mark, watching my husband take off the navy tie I helped him knot before we left for the company holiday party tonight.

He looks so good in a suit.

A soft smile plays on my lips as he slips out of his jacket.

Everything is working.

The baby. Us. Me.

Things are going so well that the cynical part of me is waiting for the other shoe to drop.

Not tonight, I think, burrowing under the covers as Andrew crosses the room, undoing his cufflinks.

Tonight was the first time I didn't drink at one of the many events Andrew is expected to attend. And every few minutes, he would look at me and smile. I knew what he was thinking. *I'm proud of you.*

And that made it all worth it.

"Did you already brush your teeth?" Andrew asks, rolling his sleeves up his forearms as he moves toward the dresser.

"Yep," I yawn, stretching under the covers. "While you were locking the house." I drop my head against the pillow. "God, I am so tired."

"Well, get your beauty rest, sweetheart. Tomorrow night we have dinner with the Waltzes. And you know how those nights go."

I groan. The Waltzes are known to keep a party going well past midnight.

Andrew opens his mouth to say something, but a cufflink slips from his fingers and rolls under the bed.

I pluck the hand lotion from the bedside table as he drops to his knees beside the bed.

And then—

Everything stops.

Sound. Movement.

With the bottle of lotion hovering over my palm, I freeze.

It takes Andrew only a second to reappear, but when he does, there's something in his hand—an *empty* wine bottle. One that I had drained in secret and had hidden during my final month of drinking.

My stomach drops.

Andrew gapes down at it.

"I didn't," I stutter. "It was just that bottle. I drank a few sips here and there to help with the withdrawals."

I expect rage. A bottle flying. A window breaking. Screaming.

Instead, Andrew sets the bottle on the bedside table, then lowers onto the edge of the bed next to me.

I lift off the pillow. "I promise you." Tears fill my eyes. "It was just that bottle. I promise—"

"Lillian, stop."

"But I—"

"Stop." His voice is calm, but measured, and this scares me more than if he had shouted.

He takes a deep breath, closes his eyes for a moment, then looks at me again.

"It's time we have a talk. A long overdue talk."

I nod, my heartbeat thudding in my ears.

"Lillian, I married you because I fell madly in love with you. I am here, today, because I am still in love with you. But you have to understand something—it hasn't been easy." His jaw twitches. "*You* haven't been easy. Your alcoholism hasn't been easy.

"When we married," he continues, "I made a vow to stand by your side. I meant that, which is why I do the things I do. Why I'm so controlling."

I barely whisper, "I don't like it, Andrew."

"I don't either," he admits. "I don't like having to watch your every move, Lillian. Believe me, I don't. I don't like having to hide your car keys every night. But you make terrible decisions when you drink. Dangerous decisions. Decisions that could kill not only you but someone else."

I flinch.

Andrew lifts his knee onto the bed and angles toward me. "I have sent you to rehab twice. I have gone to AA meetings with you. I have ordered every self-help book on the market. Nothing works. You have been fired from every job you've ever had because of your drinking—and yes, I know about you being fired recently from your volunteer work, too. Your life revolves around this addiction."

Tears pool in my eyes.

"We've lived like this for a long time. But now," he glances at my belly, "everything has changed." His voice softens. "Now I have not only you, but our baby to look out for."

He reaches for my hand. "Lillian, I need you to keep our baby healthy. I need you to be strong. And I will be here with you every step of the way."

My chin quivers. "But you're not with me all the time."

"I will be as much as I can. And when I'm not..." He gently taps my heart. "I'm right here. I'm *always* right here."

A sob bursts from my throat. I propel myself forward, wrap my arms around him, and weep into his chest.

"I love you so much," I choke out. "I don't know what I would do without you."

TWENTY-EIGHT
JACOB

I crouch low, my eyes scanning the dried sneaker prints embedded in the dirt. The surrounding ground is also disturbed, patches of earth turned up, twigs snapped underfoot. I follow the trail a few paces, careful not to step on the prints themselves. The path weaves between the trees, leading away from the crime scene, toward a small break in the brush where the undergrowth has been crushed down—possibly where they exited.

The noise of the crime scene—the media, the crowd, the chaos—is far behind me. It feels good to be alone. Peaceful. But just as quickly as the peace registers, a twig snaps behind me.

Slowly, I shift my weight, angling my body just enough to glance over my shoulder.

"Hey, Lockhart."

Officer Woodson is a few yards back, standing just off the trail with Charles, the man who found the body. Unlike when I first saw him—dazed, vacant—Charles looks vastly different now. He's flushed with adrenaline, eyes wide, hands twitching at his sides, shifting from foot to foot like he's barely containing whatever's bubbling inside him.

Woodson cups his hand to his mouth. "Can I talk to you for a second?"

Carefully, I pick my way back to the main trail, avoiding any tracks I might have missed.

"Sorry to pull your attention," Woodson says. "But I thought you should know—"

"I saw her!" Charles blurts, cutting him off. "The woman who killed Rat! She was here—she ran away when she saw us! She—"

"Just a minute, please." Woodson holds up a hand to Charles then refocuses on me. "Charles and I were on our way to retrace his steps when we noticed a woman standing next to the police tape. She looked startled when she saw us, and when Charles started yelling at her, she bolted."

"She *ran?*" I ask.

Woodson nods.

"Charles," I frown. "I got the sense that you couldn't discern any details of the person you saw. Not even if it was a man or a woman."

Charles licks his lips, rubbing his hands over his arms. His nerves are electric, jumping all over the place. "I know, man, I know I said that, but when I saw her, it was like a light bulb went off. I don't ever forget a face, I promise. Ask anyone around here. I might not remember much, but I remember your face. And it was her, man. I'm certain. She was lurking around the woods close to Rat's cabin a few days before I found him, and I ain't never seen her here before."

The problem with eye-witness accounts? They're unreliable as hell. Memories bend and twist, rewriting themselves under pressure. People swear they saw things that never happened. But Charles—high or not—believes what he's saying.

"Did you get a solid visual?" I ask Woodson, who, unlike Charles, still seems grounded in reality.

"I can do better than that. I know who she is."

My brows pop. I ask Charles to give us some space. Once he has moved out of earshot, Woodson continues.

"It was Savanna Portman."

For a moment I say nothing. I glance back at the dried boot prints in the dirt that I've been studying. Then—

"You're sure?"

Woodson nods, regarding me closely. "Positive."

I look in the direction of the crime scene, my mind racing.

"You going to go interview her?" Woodson asks.

I rub the back of my neck. "Appears so."

TWENTY-NINE
SAVI

The words on my screen begin to melt together as I read back the two chapters I've just written. I'm happy Lillian is going to help the homeless man who helped her. And now I'm craving peanut butter crackers.

Closing my eyes, I lean back. I feel better. The escape of writing combined with the pain pills have helped both my mood and headache.

What a weird, *weird*, day.

I press my palms against my eyes.

I need a break.

No—first, I need to send off the damn cozy mystery synopsis to my editor, Eliot. So I do. I hit send—and immediately feel terrible about it. I didn't even spell-check the thing. Didn't read it over. Just packaged up my ill-thought-out plot, slapped a subject line on it, and launched it into his inbox like a debut author with nothing to lose.

Feeling like I want to jump off a bridge, I push out of my chair.

Frozen yogurt. That's what I'll do. A quick trip to my favorite place. Sit, people-watch, unwind, clear the head. Then I'll go straight to my therapist's office.

. . .

Twenty minutes later, I'm pulling into the parking lot of Frozen Bliss, the only frozen yogurt place in town.

The teenage girl behind the counter barely glances up from her phone as I pay for my order at the kiosk, then grab a cup and swirl a ridiculous amount of chocolate fudge yogurt into it. Usually, I go for something fun—sprinkles, cookie crumbles, maybe a drizzle of caramel. But today, I don't bother.

I sit by the window, spooning the cold sweetness into my mouth, staring out at the tourists wandering the sidewalks. A couple passes by, peering at me through the window. I look away.

I glance over my shoulder and catch the girl at the register staring at me now. She quickly looks away when our eyes meet.

When I turn back, the couple that had just passed by the window is now inside the store and standing right next to me with beaming smiles on their faces.

The woman is the first to speak. "Excuse me—so sorry to bother you—but you're Savanna Portman, right? The author?"

I manage a polite smile, though nerves rocket through me. "Yes."

Her partner leans in slightly, his voice lowered as if we're sharing a secret. "We just love your books. Like, truly. We both read *Holy Sheet Cake!* on our honeymoon—well, not the whole time, obviously—but we were hooked."

The woman giggles and elbows him gently. "You're even more beautiful in person. I told him it was you, didn't I, Dan? I said, 'That's her, I swear it is.'"

I grip my spoon tighter, unsure what to do with my face. Smile? Laugh? Nod meaningfully?

"Would you mind signing something for us?" she asks, already digging through her oversized leather tote. "I don't have your book on me, but I've got a receipt, or—oh, wait!"

With triumphant energy, she pulls out a folded diaper—not used, thankfully—and flattens it on the table between us. "This'll do, right? It's clean. I think."

I blink at it. "Uh..."

Dan pulls out his phone. "Do you mind if we get a quick photo too? Just real fast, I promise. We'll be out of your hair in a second."

I glance over at the girl behind the counter. I think she's videoing this. Great.

"Sure," I mutter, "no problem at all."

I pick up the pen they hand me and bend awkwardly over the crinkly, plasticky diaper surface, scrawling my name across the top fold. The ink bleeds a little.

Dan leans in beside me for the photo, his arm brushing mine. I force a smile, praying to the gods above that I don't have chocolate yogurt in the corner of my lips. Which, come to think of it, would really tie in with the diaper in my hand.

My God, I am holding a diaper for a picture that I am certain will be posted on social media.

Fantastic.

"Thank you *so* much," the woman gushes, taking the diaper from my sweaty hand. "We'll let you get back to your... yogurt."

They leave as quickly as they came, chattering excitedly, the door jingling behind them.

I stare down at my cup. The yogurt has started to melt—and now my appetite is gone.

After tossing my half-eaten yogurt in the trash, I head back to the minivan, feeling more exposed than ever. More trapped in this abnormal life that is slowly becoming my normal.

I shove the van into drive and head to my therapist's office—for the second time today.

THIRTY

SAVI

It's déjà vu. Dr. Lin sits in her usual spot across from me, legs crossed, notepad balanced on her lap, pen poised. Her expression is kind but concerned.

"Thanks for squeezing me in."

"Thanks for coming."

I glance down at my jogging clothes—dusty, sweat-streaked, and clinging to me from this morning's spiral at the trail. I wonder if Dr. Lin notices the difference. Just hours ago, I sat in this very chair wearing a neatly pressed sweater and jeans, hair brushed, smile practiced. Now I look like garbage.

I make a mental note to change the moment I get home. Into something soft. Familiar. Maybe my favorite threadbare sweatpants and oversized T-shirt.

We sit in silence for a beat, the clock ticking loudly above the bookshelves. I'm fidgeting with a smooth stone from a decorative bowl nearby.

"I'm unraveling," I finally say.

Dr. Lin's pen moves across her notepad. "Tell me what that feels like."

"Like..." I pause, running my thumb rhythmically over the stone's surface.

I've already decided I'm not bringing up the weird incident at the trail. I know I'm reading too much into it, and the last thing I want is to give it more air time than it deserves. If I say it out loud, it becomes real. And right now, honestly, I feel like I can't handle my therapist doing a deep dive into it. She'd make me talk about it, analyze, and—I just can't.

"Like I'm spinning out of control," I continue. "I can't focus. I'm having headaches all the time now, and the dreams."

"And worries about sleepwalking?"

"Right." I sigh heavily. "I don't know. I just feel... off. Everything feels *really* off."

Dr. Lin folds one leg over the other. "Savi, this morning we talked about how you felt trapped in your work. I want to reiterate, this level of attention and recognition, the stress of being in the public eye—it's a powerful trigger. You were catapulted from obscurity into the spotlight. That can cause real emotional and psychological stress."

I nod, eyes flicking to the bookshelf, the edge of her desk, anywhere but her face.

"When you asked me if you've been sleepwalking, I wondered if that were in connection to the memory issues—as you call it— that we've been working on for a while now. Did something happen recently to make you think you were sleepwalking, or perhaps doing something you don't remember?"

I think about the man at the gas station, who was certain I was there, and then the man accusing me of murder. Dr. Lin's question is so leading I get the feeling that she knows what happened this morning on the trail.

We stare at each other for a moment, and for the first time, I wonder if I can truly trust her.

I don't respond.

She gives a small nod, writing something else down.

I shift in my seat.

"You mentioned the headaches." She switches gears. "Have you noticed any patterns when they come on?"

"Not that I recall, no."

"Let's put a pin in that question. I wonder if these headaches are accompanying the added anxiety you're having. Next time you get one, take a moment to jot down what happened prior to it. Let's see if there's a pattern."

Dr. Lin's phone lights up on the corner of the desk. My heart stutters when I see the name flashing on the screen:

Jacob Lockhart.

I drop the stone, sending it clattering onto the rug.

"Oops," I murmur, leaning forward to retrieve it.

When I straighten, she's already flipped the phone face down.

We hold each other's gaze for a beat too long, and I get the unmistakable feeling that Dr. Lin knows something I don't. Like I'm out of the loop on something.

Why would the homicide detective be calling my therapist?

It's not about me, I tell myself. Dr. Lin has dozens of clients.

But even as I think it, I don't believe it.

THIRTY-ONE
JACOB

It's early afternoon when I pull into the short driveway of a modest brick home on the east side of town.

Dead leaves swirl around my boots as I step out of my service vehicle. I close the door, and out of the corner of my eye, I catch movement behind a sheer curtain. A shadow shifts.

Quickly, it disappears.

I walk up the rounded brick steps to the front door, my focus flicking back to the window. The same figure appears again—this time, pink-tipped fingernails part the fabric, revealing a single, wide bloodshot eye.

The curtain drops.

I ring the doorbell.

Nothing.

I knock. Once. Twice.

"Ms. Portman, it's the police. Please open your door."

Finally, the lock clicks and the door opens just enough for me to see her.

Savanna Portman looks like a woman on the verge of collapse.

Her brown hair is piled into a messy bun, strands frizzing out at odd angles. She's wearing baggy sweatpants, and an oversized long-sleeved shirt. Her eyes—sharp and anxious—scan me with wariness.

"How may I help you?" She grips the edge of the door with fingers so tight, her knuckles turn white.

I clock her bare feet. No running shoes. Just a pair of worn Birkenstocks.

"Ms. Portman, my name is—"

"Jacob Lockhart," she says, almost breathlessly. "I know who you are."

I keep my expression neutral. "May I come in?"

She hesitates.

"I just have a few quick questions," I press. "I promise, I'll be out of your hair before you know it." I offer a disarming smile.

She wets her lips.

Another beat of hesitation.

Then, "Sure. Yeah. Come in."

Inside, the air is warm, faintly scented with freshly baked muffins. Blueberry, if my nose serves me correctly. The foyer opens into a modest living room, lived-in but neat. Everything has a place, spaced equally apart. A laundry basket sits on the coffee table next to a half-drunk glass of water and a fitness magazine promising "*Abs in 10 Days*." A pair of dehydrated ficus trees flank the bay window, their leaves dry and curled at the edges. Beyond that, a small deck overlooks a fenced-in backyard, where three large piles of leaves sit in uneven mounds. A rake leans against the railing.

Savanna grabs the laundry basket and whisks it out of sight, then snatches the water glass, hesitates, and sets it on a coaster. Nervous, erratic movements.

Pretending not to notice, I nod toward the window. "Great backyard for a dog."

Savanna frowns, then looks outside. "Oh. Yeah. I don't know."

"Not a dog person?"

Ignoring the question, she begins folding an afghan, like she needs to keep her hands busy or she might unravel.

"You know," I say, shifting the subject, "I sure could use a cup of coffee on this cold, misty day. You have any?"

She blinks at me. Then, relief flickers across her face. I've offered her a task. A distraction. A way to reset.

"Yes. Absolutely. Please, come in the kitchen."

The tension in her shoulders melts as soon as the coffee begins brewing.

I scan the small, cozy kitchen. White cabinets. Spotless fridge. Copper cookware hanging above a small island. A fruit bowl with apples and two green bananas.

No running shoes.

Savanna leans against the counter, shifting restlessly. She crosses her arms, uncrosses them. Finally, she picks up an empty mug with one hand, then grips the counter behind her with the other, bracing.

The coffee begins to spit and gurgle.

"I just have a few questions, and I'll be out of your way." I match her posture, leaning casually across from her. "Did you happen to visit Halsey Trail this morning?"

"Why do you ask?"

"I was there visiting a cabin just off the trail. Someone mentioned they saw you."

Her gaze darts to the floor.

Just be honest, I think. *Just. Be. Honest.*

"Yes," she says finally. "I went for a run this morning. And—yes—there was... a man. I didn't know him—I've never seen him before. He started screaming at me."

I nod, encouraging. "Did you run away from him?"

Her cheeks flush deep red. "Yes."

"Why?"

"Because it scared me. He was screaming wildly, and there was an officer with him, too, and he reached for his belt and I didn't know if he was going for his gun and I just—I just ran."

I nod. "That's understandable."

She exhales. "Thank you. So. What happened?"

"That's what I'm trying to understand. To be blunt, Ms. Portman, you're my first lead."

"Lead?"

"The man who saw you said he recognized you from the night of the incident. He said he saw you that night."

"When exactly?"

"I think it would have been the night before you left for your big New York trip that everyone's talking about. Around that time, anyway."

"Where did he see me?"

"In the woods, near the cabin and the encampment."

"That's impossible." Her voice sharpens and I get my first glance of the strong woman underneath that nervous exterior. "I wasn't there."

"Are you sure?"

"Why would I go in the woods in the middle of the night? Especially that area? Especially to a total stranger's cabin?"

"That's what I'm here to ask."

The flush works its way down to her neck. She's on the verge of breaking down—or lashing out.

When she doesn't speak, I continue, "Ma'am, a man was killed in his home that night. Stabbed to death, to be exact. Anything you can tell us—"

"*Stabbed* to death?" she squeaks. "I'm sorry—did you say *stabbed?*"

I nod.

Her eyes round and she stares down at the empty coffee cup in her hand. A very—*very*—long moment passes. Then, suddenly, "Oh. You wanted coffee." She turns, robotically pours two cups. Her hand trembles as she hands me one, then sets hers down untouched.

I sip, watching her over the rim. "It's good."

She's not looking at me anymore. Her stare is vacant, fixed on a spot on the floor.

"So you're sure you weren't in the woods, around the encampment?"

"Yes," her voice cracks.

"How about recently? Have you been recently?"

"No."

"What about to the trails adjacent to the cabin?"

She hesitates, but shakes her head.

"So, to confirm, you haven't been in the vicinity of the encampment in, let's say, the last week."

"Correct."

"You mean aside from this morning, when you went to the trails for a jog... right?"

"Oh. Yes, right. Aside from this morning, no."

"Well, okay then." I take another long pull of the coffee, then set down my mug. "I'll get out of your hair—actually, do you have a bathroom I can use before I head out?"

Her frown deepens. Like the request isn't processing.

Then, "Yes. Sure. This way."

Savanna leads me through the living room to a small bathroom between two bedrooms. Inside, I close the door, turn on the water, then scan the floor.

No running shoes.

Dammit.

The small vanity contains a sink, a storage space below, and a line of drawers on the side. Quietly, I check the drawers, then under the sink. All the normal things. Cleaning agents, a toilet brush, a plunger.

I flush the toilet and exit the bathroom.

Savanna is waiting for me outside the door. She leads me to the front door, eager for me to leave.

I pause as I step over the threshold and turn back to her. "By the way, do you mind if I take a look at the running shoes you wore to the trail this morning?"

Her eyes snap up to mine.

They narrow.

"Not without a warrant, Detective."

THIRTY-TWO

SAVI

My heart is still hammering as I slam shut the door. At this point, I'm certain it's going to give out if I have one more surprise today.

I stand there, frozen, listening—waiting—until I hear the crunch of twigs under Detective Lockhart's tires as he reverses out of the driveway.

Then I rush to the window, peeling back the curtain with trembling fingers. My breath fogs against the glass as I watch his unmarked car disappear down the street, swallowed by the quiet small-town normalcy of Bear's Creek.

Even then, I wait another minute to ensure he doesn't come back, like *Columbo*, the old detective show I used to watch as a little girl, when the detective always had one last question before revealing what he really knew.

Finally, I take a step back. My stomach twists so violently that I press my back against the door, sliding down to the floor in slow motion until I'm crumpled there like a rag doll.

What is happening to me?

I squeeze shut my eyes, thread my fingers through my hair, and grip my scalp.

Am I a suspect in a murder investigation?

Two people—two *separate* people—are accusing me of being in the vicinity of the cabin the night of "the incident."

Jacob Lockhart—local homicide detective—has asked for my running shoes. Because they might be connected to the murder scene.

No, I'm not a *lead,* as the detective said, I'm a *suspect*.

I pull my knees to my chest.

This is insane.

I, Savanna Portman, am linked to a murder.

How can that be?

What will this do to my career? My new contract, the book tour—my entire life—it could all disappear. Everything I've worked so hard for, gone in an instant, if I truly am a suspect. And once the media gets hold of the story, it'll be everywhere, splashed across headlines for the world to see.

Add to this that the *fictional* thriller that I write in the secret of my room appears to be playing out in *real life*.

I thought the fact that I'd written about a murder in a cabin in the woods days before a body was discovered was just a strange coincidence, but how do I explain that the victim died in the exact same manner as in my book? By *stabbing*.

And what about the other strange coincidences? Katie getting fired, and then me almost passing out on the trail, both occurring *after* I'd written similar scenes.

How many coincidences can there be before they stop being coincidences?

Could someone have read my manuscript? And this very sick person is acting out the story in real life?

No. My laptop is password protected, and besides, Katie is the only one who knows I'm secretly writing a thriller. And she certainly didn't read it.

...Right?

Moving on autopilot, I hurry to the kitchen. I yank open the cabinet, pop two more painkillers, and chug a glass of water.

Think, Savi. Think.

Call Eric? No. He's on the road and never answers the phone while he's driving. Katie? No. She's dealing with her own shit.

The police? Ha. The police are the ones accusing me.

I bend over the counter, scrubbing my hands over my face.

I should call a lawyer. But that's crazy, right? I didn't do anything wrong.

I didn't do anything wrong.

Then why is my body reacting like this? I know I'm innocent, so why am I freaking out so much?

Just then, my phone rings.

It's my editor, Eliot. He must be calling about the synopsis I sent him earlier. *God help me.*

I freeze, paralyzed in the kind of existential inaction usually reserved for deer in headlights. But the phone keeps ringing.

"Hi, Eliot!" I answer on the fourth ring, my voice three octaves too high—too fake.

"Savi. Wow. That's the most energetic I've ever heard you answer the phone." he laughs. "Am I catching you at a bad time?"

There couldn't possibly be a worse time. Instead, I chirp, "No! Not at all. I was just—uh—plotting."

"Love that," he says. "I always say the best time to reach a writer is when the wheels are turning."

Right. The only wheels turning are the ones screaming: *you're a suspect in a murder investigation.*

"So," he continues, "I've had a chance to look at the synopsis you sent over. The tea shop is a cute hook. The etiquette-obsessed Victorian ghost? Funny. Charming."

He pauses.

"But..."

Ah. There it is. The ominous *but.*

"I have to admit, this one feels a little different from your usual tone. Darker. Actually, a lot darker. The mood in the second half— Amy spiraling, the séance gone wrong, that bit about the ghost forcing her to relive her childhood trauma through mirror reflections? It's... intense."

I blink. "Right."

"I guess I'm just wondering—is this still a cozy mystery? Because I'm not sure poisoning, hallucinations, and such emotional scenes are going to feel comforting to our usual audience..."

Another pause, like he's choosing his words carefully.

"Look, it's got bones. Strong bones. But it feels like this one's wandering away from your brand. And I know you've had a whirlwind year—book tour, bestseller lists, new contracts. I just want to make sure you're okay."

That stops me.

"Oh," I say, caught off guard. "Yeah. I'm fine. Totally fine."

There's a rustle of paper on his end. "I guess my main concern is that the cozy part seems to be missing. We're usually working with charming towns and pie-eating contests and a sidekick with a penchant for matchmaking. But this feels more... I don't know. Unsettled. Like Amy's unraveling."

Because maybe she is. Because *I* am.

"I'll take another pass," I say quickly. "Lighten the tone. Refocus the arc. More cookies, less trauma. Got it."

Eliot chuckles, but it's distracted. "Good, good. Just send a revision as soon as you can, please. Marketing's eager for teasers, so ideally in the next week."

We hang up with polite goodbyes and vague optimism.

The second the call ends, I let the smile fall off my face. My fingers are still curled around the phone. My heart is still pounding.

THIRTY-THREE
SAVI

I toss my phone on the counter, nearly tripping over my own feet as I hurry to the bedroom. The sneakers I wore to the trail this morning—the ones Lockhart asked to see—are still sitting where I left them, right by the laundry hamper.

I stare down at them.

There's something at that crime scene that he thinks links to these running shoes.

I grab the sneakers, shove them into a plastic grocery bag, and yank my coat off the hook by the door. I peel out of the driveway, heading toward the lake.

I need to get rid of them. I need to get rid of whatever this is before it consumes me whole. I have a brand new career to think about. I can't let anything ruin it.

A sign ahead reads:

Table Ridge Lake—Five Miles.

The road narrows, twisting around the mountains like a snake. The lake shimmers in the distance, a vast, endless black mirror reflecting the overcast sky.

But the closer I get, the more the panic starts to turn into something else. Doubt.

My fingers tighten around the steering wheel.

What am I doing? What *the hell* am I doing?

This is not normal. Normal, innocent people don't drive to a secluded lake in the middle of the day to get rid of their shoes. Innocent people don't destroy evidence.

I swerve onto the shoulder and slam the van into park.

My forehead drops onto the steering wheel as a dry, humorless laugh claws its way up my throat. This is the moment in a thriller where the reader would scream at the protagonist: *Stop! You're being ridiculous! Turn around!*

Turn around, Savi.

"You are innocent," I whisper. "You were just in the wrong place at the wrong time. Everything is going to be okay."

Inhaling, I lift my head from the steering wheel.

I. Am. Innocent. And also, not stupid. If someone saw me dumping these shoes, I'd be in more trouble than I could get myself out of.

My gaze sharpens and suddenly, I know exactly what I need to do.

If Detective Lockhart wants my shoes, he can have them.

In fact, I'll deliver them myself.

THIRTY-FOUR
SAVI

I turn onto the long, winding driveway that leads to the Lockhart Estate. A jittery cocktail of anticipation and, honestly, a little excitement spins inside me. Seeing the house through my binoculars is one thing, but actually being here is something else entirely.

The trees are even grander up close, ancient and gnarled, their autumn colors brilliant against the brooding gray sky.

I grip the wheel tighter, my heart hammering as the estate finally comes into view.

It's even more breathtaking than I imagined. A massive, gothic-style mansion, perched on the mountainside like something out of a Brontë novel.

I roll to a stop in front of the stone pathway and exhale, trying to calm my nerves. Which is impossible because I am about to confront the man who just interviewed me for murder, and also, the man who is the inspiration for the main character in my novel.

What a mind fuck.

And beyond these doors, *her*—Quinn Lockhart. The elusive, mysterious woman who no one ever seems to see. The woman who has sparked endless questions in my mind. The woman who, in some way, has become the obsession fueling my manuscript. I wonder if Lillian, the character I've built, is even close to what she will be.

I climb out of the van, a plastic bag of running shoes clutched in one hand. Leaves swirl in the wind and for a moment, I just stand there, staring, awestruck.

What a life the Lockharts have.

Swallowing hard, I walk up the stone path, and press the doorbell. Before I can even take a breath the door swings open. He's wearing nothing but a white undershirt and gray sweatpants. His hair is tousled, his eyes dark and shadowed. He must have changed clothes the moment he got home. The sight of him like this—casual, undone—throws me. I've only ever seen him in neatly pressed suits.

"Ms. Portman?" There's no mistaking the surprise on his face.

I nod, my throat suddenly dry. "Detective Lockhart."

"Come in," he says quickly, like he's worried I'm about to bolt.

The moment I cross the threshold, it's like entering another world.

The foyer is enormous, grand and warm all at once. A massive chandelier—the size of my entire living room—hangs from the vaulted ceiling, its golden glow casting soft pools of light over the stone floors. The walls are adorned with rich fabrics and framed artwork, all perfectly curated, nothing out of place. Thick, luxurious rugs stretch across the floors, in intricate patterns.

To my left, an arched stone doorway leads into a sitting room with floor-to-ceiling windows overlooking the mountain range. A roaring fire crackles in a massive stone fireplace, bathing the furniture in flickering amber light. The deep scent of burning wood lingers in the air.

It smells like *home*.

"Wow," I breathe.

The detective shuts the door behind me. "It's gaudy and obnoxious, I know."

"No." I shake my head, turning in a slow circle, taking it all in. "It's stunning."

"Is everything okay?" he asks, concerned.

I tear my gaze away from the grandeur of the house and focus on the detective.

I square my shoulders and lift the shoes. "I wanted to give these to you."

"The running shoes I asked for earlier?"

"Yes. These were the shoes I was wearing during my jog when I came across the crime scene. The shoes you wanted to see. I didn't clean them or anything; they are in the exact same shape as when I got home from the trail. So. Here."

He takes them, then looks back at me. "What made you decide to bring them to me?"

I clear my throat and recite the words I'd practiced in the car. "Because I had absolutely nothing to do with what happened in that cabin. I got spooked when the man started screaming at me, and the cop reached for his belt. And, honestly, when you showed up at my house, it freaked me out. It took me a minute to get my head right."

Before he can respond, footsteps echo from deeper inside the house.

A woman steps into the foyer.

She stops cold when she sees me, her eyes widening slightly.

My heart stops.

This has to be her! *Quinn Lockhart.* I am finally laying eyes on the mysterious wife of Detective Lockhart.

She's beautiful. Not in the way I imagined Lillian to be while writing her, but in an entirely different way. She has smooth, glowing brown skin and dark, wavy hair that cascades over her shoulders. Her large eyes are rich and warm, her lips full and slightly parted, as if she's about to say something but isn't sure what.

She's dressed casually, in black leggings and an oversized sweater that slips slightly off one shoulder.

"Miss Portman, this is Selma Abuelo. My... friend."

I blink. *Friend?*

The tension in the room thickens, leaving zero doubt that this woman is *not* just a friend.

My gaze flickers around the space again, searching for Quinn. His *wife*.

Selma clears her throat. "Pleasure to meet you."

We shake hands.

"Miss Portman just stopped by to drop off something for the investigation."

Selma's perfectly arched brows lift slightly. "Oh?"

"Yes." I hesitate for a moment before blurting, "Is Mrs. Lockhart home?"

The detective and Selma exchange a quick glance, then he says, "She's in the bath."

Liar.

He quickly redirects the subject. "Is there anything else you'd like to talk about?"

"No, uh..." My gaze flickers to the grand staircase and I get a strong impulsive desire to sprint up the stairs and look for Quinn.

"Do you remember something else, perhaps?" he presses, regaining my attention.

"No, I just wanted to give you the shoes."

I turn to leave, but something catches my eye.

On the console table near the front door sit two innocuous objects, haphazardly placed—like someone had hurried inside and emptied their hands.

One pair of winter gloves.

And one pack of cinnamon gum.

My breath catches.

Gloves and cinnamon gum—the exact two things the gas station clerk swore *I* bought the night of the murder.

My heart rockets to my throat.

I step outside, forcing myself down the stone path, my spine straight, my gait steady. But inside, everything spins.

I *knew* it wasn't me at the gas station. The gloves, the gum— they belong to someone in *this* house.

The clerk didn't see *me* that night, he saw someone who looked like me.

My mind flits to the one person in Bear's Creek I've never actually seen, despite watching the estate like a hawk for months.

Quinn Lockhart.

Is the detective's own *wife* the real suspect he's looking for?

THIRTY-FIVE

TBD - A Thriller

Inspired by the mysterious Quinn and Jacob Lockhart of Bear's Creek.

Written by: Savanna Portman

Lillian

Andrew's foul mood permeates the cab as we back out of the garage.

Neither of us slept well after Andrew discovered the empty wine bottle I'd hidden under the bed to help with alcohol withdrawal during my first months of pregnancy.

And now we have a formal dinner to attend.

Great.

I wrap my cashmere shawl tighter around my shoulders, as if it might shield me from the tension radiating from the driver's seat. Tonight, I'm wearing a fitted midi dress, elegant and understated, that highlights my growing belly.

Outside, an endless sky blankets overhead—no moon, no stars, just inky black. The streetlights whiz past in rhythmic bursts, illuminating Andrew's clenched jaw and the white-knuckled grip he has on the wheel.

I can't take it anymore.

"Are you okay?" I ask, finally.

"Yes."

"No, you're not. We've been avoiding each other all day."

No response.

"Andrew, just talk to me. Please."

He exhales sharply through his nose. "Fine. I'm still mad about the wine. Because you were drinking while you're pregnant, Lillian. Because you made another reckless choice."

His voice has none of the calm restraint he had last night. Then, he approached the conversation with a quiet sort of sadness, like he was trying to preserve something fragile between us. But today? Today his anger is crackling just under the surface.

"I told you I'm sorry," I say, trying to keep my voice steady. "I told you I'm done drinking."

"Why should I believe that?" His eyes flash to mine, cold and cutting. "How do I know that empty bottle wasn't from last week? Or yesterday? You say a lot of things, Lillian, but none of them come with proof."

"I forgot to throw it away. I promise you, it was from the first month."

A long moment stretches between us and in that excruciating moment, anger—raging *hormones*—boil over.

I snap, "Do you regret having a child with me?"

The pause is crushing.

Tears prick my eyes, but I refuse to let them fall. "Well, I'm fucking sorry, okay? I'm sorry you're trapped in an awful loveless marriage to a loser alcoholic."

"That's not—don't say that, Lillian."

"But that's what it is, right? I've failed you so many times that you don't trust me and now you're trapped. And the worst part is that I can't do anything about it. Even if I stop drinking forever, you will always doubt me. You'll always be checking up on me. Spying. Always expecting me to slip." My voice breaks. "You know what? I can't do this anymore. I can't live like this. When we get home, I want to talk about separating."

Andrew's head snaps toward me. *"What?"*

"You don't even want this baby with me!"

"Lillian, no, this is crazy. We are not separating. Not while you're carrying—"

"The baby you wish was from another woman!" I scream.

And that's when I see it.

A flash of headlights.

Andrew's gaze darting over my shoulder.

His eyes widening in horror.

"Hang on!" he yells.

I turn my face.

Time slows as I see the car barreling toward us.

A deafening crash explodes through the night as metal collides with metal.

Glass shatters. Tires screech. My head whips violently to the side, my skull slamming into the window, then snapping forward as the car spins.

The airbag detonates with a sharp bang, slamming into my chest, knocking the breath from my lungs. I grab onto the door but my fingers slip because we're still spinning.

The car comes to a jarring halt. Everything stops.

For a moment, I sit there, dazed, ears ringing, trying to understand what just happened.

The airbag is pressed against my face. I wrestle with it as the smell of hot brakes, leaking oil, and smoke fills my nose. Somewhere in the distance, I hear screams. Loud, urgent shouting. Horns blaring.

Finally, I manage to pull the airbag to the side. The cab is filled with smoke. I begin choking, coughing.

"A—Andrew," I croak, swatting away the smoke. "Andrew!"

He's sitting perfectly upright, the airbag crumpled against his torso. His head is resting against the headrest, his eyes closed. A large gaping wound bleeds from above his eyebrow.

He's not moving.

Panic crashes over me like a tidal wave.

"Andrew!" I scream, reaching for him, but my seatbelt jerks me back.

Outside, dark silhouettes gather around the windows, their faces blurred through the smoke. Fists bang against the windows. Screams echo outside the car—urgent screaming.

I can't breathe. The smoke is intensifying.

My eyes are watering so much that I can't see anymore.

The last thing I remember is clawing at the seatbelt, trying to get to Andrew.

THIRTY-SIX

SAVI

I hear the sound of tires crunching over twigs in the driveway.

I jolt upright from my laptop, my chair scraping against the floor as I shove away from my desk.

For a fleeting moment I wonder if it's Detective Lockhart coming back to arrest me after finding something on the shoes I delivered to his house earlier.

I peek through the curtains.

Across the street porch lights flicker on and the first stars twinkle in a dimming sky. Katie's little silver Honda is parked in the driveway. She steps onto the porch carrying an autumn-colored bouquet wrapped in white paper.

The tension in my shoulders drains. Thank *God*.

I swing open the door before she even has a chance to insert her key.

"God I'm glad you're home. It's been a hell of a day."

"I had a feeling," she lifts the arrangement in her hand, "so I brought flowers."

"You're not going to believe this." I grab her free hand and drag her to the kitchen. "I got you flowers, too. This morning, at the grocery store, after we spoke." I gesture dramatically to the bouquet of roses I bought for her earlier, resting on the counter. "I'm so sorry about the job."

"Oh, Savi, that's so sweet of you. Thank you."

I fall into her embrace. There's a faint trace of wine on her breath.

I hold her tight for a second longer than normal.

I needed this. Flowers. Her.

"Why did you get *me* flowers?" I ask, pulling away.

"Something just told me do it." She winks. "And I figure you're upset about Eric leaving so soon again. Come on, let's get these in water."

I follow Katie to the kitchen. "Tell me everything about getting fired. What happened exactly?"

Katie sets down the flowers and grabs scissors from the drawer. "There is truly nothing to talk about. And honestly, I really don't want to rehash it. Trust me, I've been thinking about it all damn day."

I hand her a vase, and she begins cutting the stems as I lean against the counter, mirroring the exact stance I had when Detective Lockhart was here earlier.

"How about you talk to me?" she says. "Tell me what's got you looking ghostly pale?"

"I don't even know where to start," I admit.

"Just start talking, I'll piece it together."

I chew my lip, watching her trim the flowers. The sharp *snip snip* of the scissors against the stems feels oddly therapeutic. She strips the lower leaves and drops them into the sink, then begins arranging the bouquet in water.

I begin. "Okay, so you know how when we talked this morning, I was on my way to the grocery store, then the trails for a jog?"

"Uh-huh," she says, inspecting a sunflower and adjusting its angle before dropping it into the vase.

"Well, I stopped for gas, and the guy behind the counter swore up and down that I was there a few nights ago—in the *middle of the night*."

Katie stills, looking over her shoulder. "Wait, what?"

"He said he remembers because I made a bet with him over a football game. But I wasn't even there."

Katie frowns and turns back to the flowers, rotating the vase as she arranges them, her face drawn in thought. "That's weird. Keep going."

"He was certain it was me. He said while I was there, I bought a pair of winter gloves and a pack of cinnamon gum."

Katie tilts her head. "And you're sure you didn't go to the gas station in the middle of the night?"

I level her with a look.

"Okay... so, he has you confused with someone else."

"Exactly! But then—" I exhale sharply, gripping the counter. "I go to the trail, and I come across a crime scene."

Katie's brows lift, but she doesn't look totally surprised. "I already heard about it," she says, snipping another stem.

"You did?"

"It's all over town. Rumor is a man was stabbed to death. Everyone's talking about it." She drops the last flower into place. "Okay, go on."

I tell her everything—about the homeless man screaming at me, accusing me of murder. About the panic, the way I ran. And finally, about Detective Lockhart showing up at my door hours later.

When I finish, Katie carefully sets down the scissors and turns to face me fully.

"Are you *kidding* me?"

"I wish."

"Hang on, honey, I'm gonna need a drink for this." She grabs a beer from the fridge, and cracks it open on the counter in one smooth motion.

She takes a long pull and then waves her hand for me to continue.

I tell her about the detective's visit. About the way he asked to see my shoes, and how I decided to drive the shoes to him later.

"I... don't remember that."

A beat of silence ticks between us.

"That's okay," she says gently, pen moving against the paper. "Memory blocks are common for you when you're overwhelmed, we've established this. And especially under stress."

The way she emphasizes the last word, *stress*, makes me wonder: Does she know I'm possibly a suspect in the Midnight Slaughter?

Dr. Lin tilts her head, regarding me closely. "The news has been heavy this week," she says, almost casually. "Everyone in town's been shaken. The man who was killed—the one they found in the woods?"

I nod, keeping my expression neutral.

"It's a lot," she continues, her voice soft. "Even if you didn't know him, events like that can rattle our sense of safety. They can trigger deeper things we're already carrying."

When I don't indulge in the conversation, she shifts gears. "I want to try something new today. A grounding technique that can be helpful when you feel disconnected."

"Okay," I say, relieved to be off the subject of murder.

Dr. Lin leans over and pulls a box from the shelf. Inside are five small objects. A feather, a piece of smooth granite, a small bottle of peppermint oil, a tiny music box, and a velvet pouch filled with beads.

"These are sensory grounding tools," she explains. "Each one engages a different sense. The goal is to gently bring your awareness back to the present. Can I show you?"

I nod.

She holds out the feather first, brushing it lightly across her wrist. "This is for touch. Something soft, repetitive. Helps settle the nervous system."

Next, she opens the oil and lets me smell it. The sharp, clean scent cuts through the fog in my head like sunlight through smoke.

Then the granite stone—cool and heavy. "This is for weight. To remind you of your body. Where you are. That you're safe. That you are *not* trapped."

I turn it over in my hand, grounding into its firmness.

"And this," she says, winding up the music box, "is sound."

It plays a gentle, tinkling melody I don't recognize, but something about it tugs at the fringes of my memory. Like I've heard it before—but I haven't.

Out of nowhere, a stabbing headache flares between my temples. My hands tighten around the stone. I close my eyes only to be met by a flash—not a thought, not a dream, but an image. The hazy outline of a chain-link fence. My feet crunching over gravel. Dusk settling in. The sharp smell of freshly cut grass.

A baseball field.

I blink hard. The image vanishes as quickly as it came.

"These items can help when you feel yourself slipping," she continues.

I meet her gaze. "Why are you giving me these now?"

She studies me. Her eyes don't blink for a long time.

"Because I think you're at a crossroads, Savi," she says, "and I want you to feel supported."

My hands tighten even harder around the stone. Her tone is almost ominous in the way she speaks. Then, she says, "I'd like to start seeing you every other day, okay?"

At the end of the appointment, Dr. Lin reminds me to keep the items with me at all times. I promise I will and step outside into the late afternoon air, with the music box melody still echoing faintly, and the pain between my temples throbbing.

THIRTY-EIGHT
SAVI

I drive home from Dr. Lin's office, my fingers tight around the steering wheel and my mind racing.

A baseball field. A chain-link fence. The sound of gravel crunching beneath my shoes.

Why?

Why a baseball field?

I've never played. I've never even been to a game, at least not one I can remember. So why did that one image—so sudden and so vivid—feel more like a memory than a dream?

Was it something I've forgotten? A buried memory?

And why did the music box trigger it?

By the time I pull into the driveway, the headache's dulled, but the unease hasn't. And because I never—*ever*—seem to catch a break these days, my phone alerts me to a virtual interview in thirty minutes.

I've done a dozen interviews in two weeks, and every single one of them has made me break out in a cold sweat—but this one takes the cake. It's a live-streamed interview with one of the top book bloggers on social media.

I race into my bedroom, pull myself together as best I can, then slip behind my laptop camera.

"Okay, we're live in five, four, three…"

I quickly smooth my blouse and check that my hair still looks presentable. Underneath the desk I'm wearing a thong and one sock.

"Hi everyone!" the host chirps. Bright-eyed, charismatic, perfectly highlighted. "Welcome back to The Cozy Crime Club—your weekly fix for all things mystery and muffins. And today, I'm so excited because we have with us *the* Savi Portman! Author of the bestselling *Holy Sheet Cake!*, her recent *New York Times* bestseller!"

Cue applause. (Literally. There's a sound effect.)

I smile, cheeks aching. "Thank you for having me."

She beams. "Savi, first of all, congratulations. Your debut cozy has totally blown up. I mean, we're talking indie bookstores, airport shelves, fan merch, people naming their cats after your characters—did you ever imagine this would happen?"

"Absolutely not," I laugh, sliding into the role of professional author.

It's becoming harder and harder.

"Honestly, I still don't really believe it's happening. I keep waiting for someone to jump out from behind a curtain and tell me it's all an elaborate prank."

She gasps. "No way! You deserve all of this. Readers are obsessed with Amy and Sheriff Higgins. Obsessed! So—obvious question—when's the next book coming out?"

Here it is. The question I knew was coming and still somehow feel wildly unprepared for.

I glance down at the blank legal pad beside me. The one that was supposed to have at least five plot points scrawled on it by now.

"Oh, you know," I say, smiling just a touch too wide. "Soon. I'm working on it now."

The host claps her hands. "Amazing! Can you tell us anything about it? Even a little teaser?"

I sip from an empty mug. "Let's just say Amy finds herself in a whole new kind of batter-related trouble. New town, new cast of quirky characters... and of course, plenty of baked goods."

"Eeeeek!" she squeals. "That sounds so fun. I can't wait."

My smile twitches. "Me too."

"And I *have* to ask—because readers are dying to know—do you really bake all those recipes from your books?"

My laugh is genuine this time. "Absolutely not. My best friend Katie is the baker. I'm a disaster in the kitchen. I have a fire extinguisher mounted next to the stove just in case."

She throws her head back laughing. "That makes me love you even more."

I shift in my seat, trying not to let the rising tide of anxiety show on my face. My foot taps under the desk, crunching on a rogue Cheerio I don't remember dropping.

I get the sudden intense urge to run. Just lunge out of my chair and run away. Literally.

"So," she says, leaning in like she's about to ask something juicy, "I noticed you *just* joined social media. What took you so long?"

I wince. "Oh... that was a publisher mandate. Apparently, it's now illegal to sell books without at least three platforms."

She giggles. "You're doing great!"

"Am I?"

She cackles. "You're hilarious! Honestly, your awkwardness is so relatable. I love that you're not one of those polished influencer types. You're real. It makes your books feel even more special."

I nod, because what else can I do? I've built an entire public persona around light-hearted small-town sleuthing and comical cake disasters. Meanwhile, the real me can barely leave the house without running through three worst-case scenarios and an escape plan.

The interview winds down with a rapid-fire round of reader questions, most of which are about Amy's love life or what flavor cupcake I'd be.

Finally, after what feels like hours, the host signs off with a cheerful, "We'll see you next time on the Cozy Crime Club!"

I wait a beat, then close the laptop and slump forward, dropping my forehead to the desk.

THIRTY-NINE

SAVI

I've forced myself to take a break from writing and am in the garage preparing for the sale we're having next month.

Katie is out job hunting.

It's unbelievable how much junk accumulates over the years. Useless trinkets that once held sentimental value. Boxes filled with old paperbacks, passed down through generations.

A smile tugs at my lips as I pull out a Nancy Drew mystery, flipping through the pages before setting it aside. Beneath it, my entire *Babysitters Club* collection is stacked in neat rows. God, I loved those books.

Tucked underneath them is a yellowed newspaper folded in half, the edges brittle and curling. I unfold it carefully, scanning the bold headline sprawled across the front page: *Bear's Creek High Wrestling Team Wins State Championship!* A grainy black-and-white photo of teenage boys in matching singlets beam up at me, their arms slung over each other's shoulders in victory.

I shake my head, half-smiling at the town's priorities. Flipping through the pages, I glance at the articles, the ads, the classifieds—until something else catches my eye. Buried beneath an ad for half-price milk at the corner store is a small, unassuming column.

Except it's only the headline. The column itself has been cut out of the paper. The headline reads: *Local Girl Missing for Three Days —No Leads in Ongoing Investigation.*

A feeling of deep sadness grips me. Tragedy has no boundaries —no respect for space or time. Horrible things happened decades ago, and they will continue to happen long after I'm gone.

Exhaling, I fold the paper and set it aside, brushing the dust from my hands.

I reach further down and pull out a gallon-sized plastic bag filled with old photographs. A few of them are Polaroids, the kind that need to be shaken out after taking.

They're all of Eric and his family. Baby pictures, school photos, the awkward pre-teen years. And then—one of him in college. He's perched on a retaining wall, a beer in one hand, a cigarette in the other, smiling that wide, carefree grin I fell in love with. His hair was longer then, always a little messy, his T-shirt slightly wrinkled.

A wave of warmth spreads over my chest. I run my fingertips over the glossy surface of the photograph, tracing the contours of his face.

We were just kids back then. We had no idea what life had in store for us. No idea that we'd get married. That we'd struggle to have a child. That we'd spend most of our adulthood pinching pennies until a crazy twist of fate would take my career soaring.

What a ride.

Tears sting my eyes. I try to swallow back the sudden rush of emotion, but the floodgates open before I can stop them.

Teardrops fall onto the photos, darkening the edges, smudging the ink.

It takes me five full minutes to pull myself together.

I stuff the photos back into the bag, shoving everything into the storage box.

I don't know why I'm so emotional. They're just old pictures of Eric.

I need to shake this off.

Pushing to my feet, I grab a couple of trash bags filled with things we don't need, and march out to the curb. The blue plastic trash can sits against the house, next to the garage door, waiting for pickup tomorrow morning.

I lift the lid, toss the bags inside, and notice something small and soft at the bottom. Purple and white.

I squint down into the can, trying to make sense of what I'm looking at.

The trash bag blocks part of my view, so I tip the can forward onto its side. The scent of stale coffee grounds and spoiled leftovers drifts into the air.

I grab a stick, reach inside, and drag the objects into the open.

It's a pair of fuzzy, purple leopard-print baby booties.

I stare at them, frowning. I don't own these. I never have.

So how did they get in our trash?

Where did they come from?

Maybe Katie left them? Maybe some kid dumped them? Maybe it's—

I gasp.

I snatch up the booties and bolt inside.

My fingers shake wildly as I wake my laptop from sleep, clicking into my manuscript, scrolling furiously.

When I find the chapter I'm looking for, my jaw slowly unhinges.

Lillian—

… But my eyes are locked on the cutest pair of fuzzy, purple leopard-print baby booties… I step inside and buy my baby her very first gift.

The *exact* booties I wrote about in my fictional manuscript—*days ago*—are now here. In real life. In my trash can.

I stumble back from the desk.

There is no way I can call this a coincidence anymore.

My manuscript is coming to life.
This isn't random.
This isn't a coincidence.
Something is happening.
I just don't understand what.

FORTY

SAVI

Desperate for answers, I find myself steering the van toward the only place I can think of: Halsey Trail. The place where everything started—or ended, depending on how you look at it.

I don't know what I'm looking for, or who I'm looking for, but I am now certain *something* is happening and I can't just sit around and ignore it anymore. I can't keep pretending what's happening between my manuscript and real life is a coincidence. I need to walk the same steps my fictional character, Lillian, walked. I need to retrace the night she murdered a man in a cabin. I need to understand how *I* knew it was going to happen before it did.

Not surprisingly, the gravel parking lot is empty. Not many people want to hike where someone was just stabbed to death.

I open the door and step into the cool autumn air.

I don't have my sneakers anymore, since I gave them to the detective, so I'm wearing an old pair of hiking boots that have sat in my closet for years. The stiff leather cracks slightly as I make my way to the trailhead.

It's quiet. No birds. No rustling of small animals in the underbrush. It's like everything knows someone died here recently.

Despite the simmering nerves, I press on, the path narrowing as I reach the footpath that veers off the main trail toward the encampment and Rat's cabin.

The crime scene tape flutters in the breeze, a garish yellow against the earthy browns and greens.

I hesitate, looking over my shoulder, then step over the tape.

Trash clings to the brambles—plastic bags caught in the low-hanging branches, beer cans half-buried in the dirt, a single, mud-streaked sneaker with no match. I move carefully, scanning the area, trying to see it as Detective Lockhart would.

What am I even looking for though?

"Want a strawberry?"

I startle, almost jumping out of my skin.

A man I hadn't noticed sits wedged between two bushes on a rolled-up tarp, his body blending into the foliage. His tattered brown coat is zipped to his throat, sleeves frayed, his gloves missing the tips of his fingers. A long, jagged scar snakes through the empty socket where his left eye should be.

In his hand, resting on his knee, is a strawberry. Rotten and oozing. It's covered in a sticky white powder.

I swallow. "No, thank you."

"You sure? It'll take you on a wild ride."

"I'm already on one, trust me."

I sidestep him carefully, resisting the urge to walk faster.

The wind picks up as I pass the encampment. Unlike the last time I was here, the place feels abandoned. Except for the two men sitting outside a tent, shuffling a deck of cards.

They glance up as I approach.

"You don't belong here, lady."

"I know."

"Then why are you?"

"I'm trying to prove I'm innocent."

The man closest to me snorts, slapping a card down onto the makeshift table between them. "Good luck."

"Do either of you know where a man named Charles is?"

The second rolls a cigarette between his fingers. "Why?"

"He accused me of something I didn't do. I'd like to talk to him."

Neither of them answer.

Fine.

I cut through the woods, finally arriving at the backyard of the cabin.

My stomach coils. It's like I've walked through the looking glass and stumbled into a scene I *created*. A sick wave of déjà vu rolls over me, stronger than anything I've ever felt before.

This is the *exact* layout from my manuscript. The trees. The trashy yard. The cabin's crooked silhouette. The path leading up behind it. I know this place—but only because I wrote it. In a *fictional* manuscript no one else has read.

Lillian walked through the woods.

Lillian came up the backside of a remote cabin.

Lillian stabbed a man to death.

And now... here I am.

A dull roar fills my ears. It's impossible, and yet I feel like I've been inserted into the bones of my own story, like I'm not Savi Portman anymore. I'm her—Lillian.

This isn't just eerie. It's terrifying.

I reach into my coat pocket and curl my fingers around the tiny, fuzzy baby booties. The same booties I had written about before finding them in my real-life trash can.

My steps slow as I maneuver around the trash in the yard. My legs feel stiff all of a sudden. Every step forward feels heavier than the last, as if my body is telling me to stop, as if it knows something my brain doesn't.

But I keep going.

Because the story is already in motion now. And somehow, impossibly, I'm caught in the middle of it.

The porch groans as I climb the warped steps, each one threatening to give under my weight.

I reach the door. It's slightly ajar.

My heart hammers against my ribcage.

Ignoring the crime scene tape, I push open the door with the toe of my boot. A waft of cold, stagnant air hits me in the face, thick with the sour scent of mildew, rot, and decay.

I duck under the yellow tape. My foot catches on the edge of the sagging threshold, and I stagger forward, catching myself on the wall. My eyes sweep the interior.

The mattress in the corner is soaked black with dried blood. I can see the indent where the body lay before it was taken to the morgue. Dark, dried splatters stretch up the walls like abstract paint strokes—chaotic and violent.

My heart feels like it's about to burst out of my chest.

I take another step into the room, but suddenly, a piercing pain slices between my temples—sharp and blinding, like someone's shoved a red-hot spike through my skull.

I stagger, one hand flying to my forehead, the other gripping the nearest piece of wall to steady myself.

My stomach lurches.

Another migraine.

The edges of the room blur. The light shifts. I drop to a crouch, gripping my knees, trying to keep myself from collapsing entirely.

I hear footsteps outside. Feel a presence.

Someone is behind me.

My head tells me to turn and protect myself from whoever is entering the cabin but the pain is so severe that all I can do is brace against it.

FORTY-ONE

SAVI

"Hey—you okay?"

The voice behind me barely registers.

"Savi? Savi—*shit*. I'm going to pick you up, okay?"

The next thing I know, I'm lifted into the air, eyes squeezed shut from the pain. The sensation is strangely weightless, like I've died and I'm drifting through space.

A steady grip holds me in place—strong, unyielding. He smells like aftershave and pine, a crisp, earthy scent that stirs a memory just outside my grasp.

A strange sense of safety wraps around me like a warm blanket. Whoever is carrying me, I trust them.

I'm carried outside the cabin.

I open my eyes. The trees above shift in blurred streaks of green and brown. I force my head off the man's chest and look up.

It's Detective Jacob Lockhart. His face is partially concealed in shadow, but I can make out his sharp jaw, the faint crease between his brows.

Oh, *shit*. This does *not* look good. Here I am, lurking around the crime scene in which he considers me a suspect.

I try to push against his chest, try to get down, but my limbs feel like lead.

"Put me down, please," I mumble.

"No."

"I can walk," I insist.

"I don't think you can."

"It's just a migraine." I close my eyes again, willing away the pounding in my skull. "I'm fine."

"You're not fine."

"Seriously. I—"

"Stop," he demands, his voice firm. "Don't argue with me when you can barely hold your own head up."

I swallow the retort on the tip of my tongue. Because he's right. I'm certain I couldn't walk on my own at this moment. So I surrender, and before long, the warmth of his grip, the steady rise and fall of his breath—it all lulls me into an uneasy calm.

And I get the strangest feeling I've been here before.

Not in the woods, but against his chest.

FORTY-TWO
SAVI

The truck jerks to an abrupt stop, sending another sharp pang through my skull. My head feels like it's been cracked open and stuffed with hot coals.

The engine cuts off. The world around me stills.

The passenger-side door swings open.

"I'm going to lift you out of the car." Detective Lockhart's voice is low and steady. And very concerned.

I try to respond, to shake my head, to tell him I can get out on my own, but I can't. The pain has stripped away my ability to do anything but exist in this raw, vulnerable state. Even the smallest movement sends shockwaves of agony. I feel weak and helpless—a sensation I detest.

His arms slide beneath me.

I let out a small, involuntary whimper as my body shifts, the movement sending another nauseating jolt through my body. But he's careful, supporting my weight as if I weigh nothing at all, cradling me against his chest as he steps away from the car.

I peek through my fingers.

The Lockhart Estate.

"Wh—what? Why am I here?"

"My house was the closest," he answers simply.

I'm here again, for the second time in a matter of days.

The detective carries me through the grand entrance. The air inside is warm and comforting. I can hear the soft hum of instrumental music drifting through the space, so faint it feels like it's part of the house itself.

And again, I get the same feeling I had the first time I was here. It feels like *home*.

Jacob moves effortlessly through the house, his grip on me strong, steady. I look around for Quinn, his wife, but there is no sign of her.

I close my eyes once again.

Then, I'm being lowered. The cool leather of a recliner presses against my overheated skin, sending a brief moment of relief. A soft *click*, then the chair shifts, reclining just enough to take the pressure off my throbbing head.

A blanket is draped over me, tucked around me like a child.

Footsteps approach.

"Honey? What's—oh no."

I recognize the voice. Selma. His mistress.

"Can you get me her migraine medicine," the detective asks, "and some water, and put on some tea, please?"

Her migraine medicine? Why would Detective Lockhart have *my* migraine medicine?

Selma hesitates. "Yes. Is she okay?"

"Yes, I think. And get an ice pack for her eyes."

Selma doesn't ask any more questions. Footsteps retreat, moving quickly down the hall.

I should be embarrassed. *I am* embarrassed. But mostly I'm disconcerted by how easily the detective is taking care of me, as if he's done it before. And also, how I feel like I've been here many times before.

A moment later, I hear Selma returning, the sound of her hurried footsteps echoing through the vast space.

"Here," she says, her voice clipped. Then she's gone again.

Detective Lockhart moves beside me. His presence is both grounding and unsettling all at once.

"Savi," he says gently, "I've got some medicine I need you to take, and then I'm going to put an ice pack over your eyes, okay?"

Savi? He just called me by my nickname.

How does the detective know my nickname?

His hand supports the back of my head as he places two pills on my tongue. I swallow them with a sip of water. Then, he gently eases me back down.

A second later, the ice pack is placed over my eyes.

A blessed relief.

And that's when I realize something.

I *have* been here before. Not just in this house. But here—in this exact room, in this exact chair. With this pain. With *him* taking care of me.

Déjà vu slams into me as hard as when I approached the cabin in the woods.

This isn't the first time I've been here, in this exact position.

I just don't remember it.

FORTY-THREE
SAVI

I don't know how long passes until I'm finally able to open my eyes. I remove the ice pack, now warm, and set it on my stomach. Whatever medicine Detective Lockhart gave me helped tremendously.

Blinking, the scene around me comes into view. I'm in what appears to be a den with dark stone walls and windows that are covered with luxe velvet curtains. Potted plants are everywhere, pulling in the connection to nature throughout the home. It reminds me of a cave, where one might spend soggy, cold Sundays curled on the couch, binge reading books.

The detective is standing over me, arms crossed over his chest, a concerned look on his face. I get the sense he hasn't left my side. Selma is behind him.

Still no Quinn.

I try to sit up, but wince.

"Stop, I'll get it."

Lockhart presses a button hidden on the side of the recliner, and slowly, I'm lifted.

I take a deep breath. "Thank you."

"Feeling better?"

"Yes. What happened?"

"Savi…" He pauses for so long that my internal red flag rises. "We need to have a serious talk."

A *serious talk?*

Selma takes a step back, to allow for privacy, though doesn't leave the room. Her face draws downward with such sadness and sympathy that nerves rocket my stomach.

I look back at Detective Lockhart.

"Savi… I need to tell you something…"

My heart suddenly feels like it's about to burst out of my chest.

"I'm your brother."

FORTY-FOUR

SAVI

The statement is so far out of left field it doesn't even penetrate. For a moment, I just stare at him.

I'm your brother.

"No." I shake my head. "No, that's—you're wrong."

The detective doesn't react. He just watches me with those cool, assessing eyes. The ones that, suddenly, seem eerily familiar.

I'm your brother.

I blink, a flicker of something buried deep in my conscious beginning to stir. A long-forgotten memory from my childhood. A whisper of another life, another time.

"This isn't funny." I press my palms into the armrests of the recliner, trying to ground myself from the panic bubbling up.

Detective Lockhart kneels down in front of me. "Savi, I wouldn't joke about this. I know it's a shock. But I need you to listen. We have a lot to talk about now."

Selma shifts beside him. Tears of pity swim in her eyes.

She knows. *She knew already.*

"I don't have a brother," I insist. "I would know if I had a brother. I grew up with my grandparents... I..." As I'm speaking, I feel the doubt in my own words. A void in my memory.

I'm not remembering something.

Why?

What *the hell* is happening?

"Savi," he continues, his voice softer now, "your maiden name is Savanna Lockhart."

"*No.*" I shake my head violently, reigniting the headache. "That's—that's Quinn's last name. That's *your* last name. That's..." My voice cracks. "This doesn't make sense. This isn't funny."

"Trust me, I'm not joking. It's a long story and it all started when you were taken from us when you were six years old."

The moment the words come out of his mouth, pops of memories flash behind my eyes.

A warm summer day. The sounds of baseballs cracking against a bat in the distance.

A hand gripping mine.

A scream.

My scream.

Shocked frozen, I stare at the detective—really look at him for the first time. The strong jawline. The high cheekbones. The slight arch in his brow when he's deep in thought. The way his lips press together when he's bracing himself, like he's doing now. The way his hands are tight fists—just like I do when I'm overwhelmed. Even the way he carries himself, the rigid posture, the ever-present alertness—it's me.

Goosebumps ripple my skin.

The proof is right in front of me. Not just in his words, but in his face. In *our* face.

"What are you talking about?" I ask, but I'm not really asking it. Because somewhere, somehow, deep down, in a way that I can't explain, I am absolutely certain that what this man is saying is true.

FORTY-FIVE
JACOB

I watch as Savi processes the last few minutes. Her hands curl into fists on her lap, her fingertips gripping the blanket like it's the only thing tethering her to reality. I want to reach for her, hold her, tell her it's going to be okay, but I know better. Right now, everything she thought she knew is crumbling around her, and there's nothing I can do to soften the fall.

She has to face this. And she has so—*so*—much more coming. We haven't even begun to scratch the surface.

I knew this day would come, and I thought I'd be prepared.

I was wrong.

"Talk," she whispers.

I take a slow breath—steadying myself.

"At six years old, you were kidnapped. You were gone for three days. One moment you were at the baseball park, the next, gone."

She gasps.

"What?"

"I had a vision..." Her eyes pop. "A flashback about a baseball park."

I nod. Her memory is slowly coming back.

She shakes her head and waves her hand at me to continue.

"Mom lost her mind, she was so worried. The whole town was

out searching for you. They put out an Amber Alert, posters, news stories. Everyone was looking. But you were just... gone."

Savi blinks in rapid succession. She's remembering little pieces, I can see it.

"And then, three days later, a ransom letter arrived. Our very rich grandparents," I gesture to the room, "whose home this used to belong to, paid the ransom. The next day someone called the tip line and said they saw someone who resembles you in Miller Park. Alone. Wandering like you'd just been dropped there."

Savi's lips part slightly, but she doesn't speak.

"You didn't remember anything. Not the person who took you. Not where you'd been. Not how you got there. Just... nothing. You were only six." I exhale, shaking my head. "We thought it was all over, and that everything was going to be okay. But it wasn't."

"You weren't the same after that," I say quietly. "It started with nightmares. Then panic attacks, really bad ones. For years. And then one day, it was like you just... shut down."

Savi grips the arms of the chair, her knuckles white. "Did anyone get me help?"

"Yes," I nod. "You saw many doctors. Therapists. Psychologists. They said it was PTSD. Dissociation. Repression. Mom tried everything to help you—until she just gave up."

"What do you mean?"

I take a deep breath. "Mom had had her own demons, ever since Dad died not long after you were born. She started drinking day and night to cope. She was paranoid all the time. She thought whoever took you was watching. That they'd come back."

Savi's eyes snap back to mine. "Did they?"

"No. The man was eventually caught, charged, arrested, and he died in jail. He'd kidnapped three other girls across three states, for ransom money. You were a target because of our grandparents' wealth. But he's dead now, Savi. Dead for a long time. You don't ever have to worry about him again."

A faint wave of relief crosses her face. "Then what happened?"

"Eventually Mom got so bad that she couldn't care for herself, let alone us, so eventually, we moved in with Grandma and Grandpa, here."

"So that's why this house feels so familiar."

"Yes. It was your home for many years. Then, in your mid-teens things got really bad. The doctors think puberty triggered it. You started lashing out, uncontrollably. Having huge blocks in memory, about everyday events, about me, your own personal information. About what happened to you. You were confused constantly, and that made you really irritated and frustrated. A few days after your eighteenth birthday, we woke up, and you had moved out. Got a tiny studio apartment across town."

"Later it got worse. You started calling yourself different names, acting really out of character, and then not remembering any of it. You spoke with an English accent some days, others Scottish. Somedays you didn't know who I was, other days you'd get really angry with me, sometimes even aggressive. The therapist said you were projecting your trauma on me because you associated me with the past, with the trauma that you couldn't remember. Years later, you erased me completely." I pause. God this is heavy. "Eventually you were diagnosed with dissociative identity disorder, a side effect of the trauma you'd never properly processed when you were young."

Savi's eyes pop open. "You mean like *multiple personalities?*"

I nod. "You live two completely different lives. Ninety percent of the time you are Savanna Portman, where you spend your days writing books and kicking ass on the *New York Times* bestseller list." I smile. She doesn't. "That's the life you believe is your only reality."

"But that *is* my real life. That *is* my reality. My house, my husband—"

"Yes, that's where you are, Savi. You married Eric Portman seven years ago. That's why your last name is Portman."

"Wait." She frowns. "Am I Savi right now?"

"Yes. Like I said, you are Savi most of the time."

"When am I *not* Savi?"

"We call them manic episodes. They happen any time you feel trapped—like you were trapped after being kidnapped. The episodes have been increasing in frequency lately, and I believe it's because of your newfound fame. You feel trapped in this new career. Trapped in the spotlight, obligations, deadlines."

"Does anyone else know?"

I nod slowly. I've been dreading this question.

"Everyone here, in town, knows what happened when you were a child, and knows you suffer psychological trauma from it. A handful of people know the real diagnosis. Savi, Bear's Creek has always looked after you. The people here, they love you. We all do. Nobody talks to you about it because they understand it would only confuse and hurt you. They're not trying to deceive you. They're trying to protect you. You've probably noticed how people are overly kind to you. How they make little accommodations. How no one questions you when you forget something—when you don't remember doing something. It's because they know and they love you."

Selma, who's been quiet this whole time, steps forward. Her voice is soft, full of warmth. "Savi... you have no idea how loved you are." She kneels beside me, her hand resting gently on Savi's knee. "This town—your friends, your neighbors, even strangers—look out for you. You are surrounded by people who would do anything for you."

I nod. "We created a life where you can exist without being tormented by your disorder and the gaps in your memory."

"So—so my entire life is a lie?"

"No." I shake my head firmly. "Your life is real, Savi. Every moment you've lived is real. It's just different."

Suddenly, horror pales her face. "Oh my God—does my agent know? Does my editor know?"

"No. They don't know anything about it."

She blows out a sigh of relief. Then, "Wait. Why hasn't anyone in town sold the news to the press, now that I've become famous?"

"Because Savi, this town has watched you grow up, watched

the fallout of the kidnapping. They are so protective of you, no matter what you do or don't do. You are like everyone's daughter, everyone's little sister."

Selma adds, "Also, it doesn't hurt that your brother is in law enforcement. If anyone talked, they know there would be hell to pay. They know you are family. There was one time a group of teens threatened to say something. Your brother took them for a long drive on the backroads and they never said a word after that." Selma winks at me, then squeezes Savi's knee gently. "I know this is a lot. And I know you feel lost right now. But you aren't lost, Savi. You have us. You always have."

Savi wipes her eyes. "And you?" She sniffs, looking at Selma. "You're Jacob's mistress?"

Selma stiffens.

"No, Savi. Selma is my wife."

"Yes," Selma gives her a sad smile. "I'm Jacob's wife. I always have been. You think Quinn is his wife, but in reality, I am." Her gaze flickers to me.

"Wait." Savi holds up a hand. "So then... who is Quinn?"

FORTY-SIX
JACOB

My throat tightens. *God, how do I say this?*

I look my sister in the eye, my chest aching. "Your other identity resides here, with me. When you are here, you believe you are my wife, Quinn."

"*What?*" Savi squeaks, her eyes rounding in horror.

"Quinn is your other personality. She's who you become when you have a manic episode. When you are Quinn, you show up at this house, likely because your memories are pulling you here, and you're convinced that you are my wife and your name is Quinn."

Selma adds softly, "When you come here, when you're having an episode, Jacob takes care of you and you sleep in the master bedroom, and Jacob sleeps with me in a room on the other side of the house, where I've hidden myself away. If it looks like you're going to be here awhile, I retreat to an apartment we purchased long ago for this very reason. I never interfere. Because in your mind, I can't exist. If I were here, it would cause too much confusion."

Savi slowly places her trembling hand over her mouth as she stares at us with huge, wild eyes.

She stays like that for a full minute.

The silence in the room is deafening.

I watch the realization bloom across her face—the horror, the recognition, the terror of knowing that her entire existence is not what she thought it was.

Selma stands and steps back, giving Savi space.

"I know this is impossible to hear," I say, having to rein in my own emotions. "But it's the truth. You don't remember because that's the nature of your disorder. You don't have access to those memories. It's like a wall goes up between your identities. When you're here, you don't know about Savi. And when you're Savi, you don't remember being here, as Quinn. You take very strong sleeping pills at night, and in the morning, everything resets."

She stares at me like a deer in headlights. It breaks my fucking heart.

Finally, breathlessly, she says, "That's why Katie is so diligent about making sure I take my sleeping pill at night and supplements in the morning. But they're not supplements, are they?"

"No. It's many different kinds of medication for your disorder." I rub the back of my neck, forcing myself to keep going. "When you come here, it's always the same pattern. You show up after something triggers you, usually in an emotional downward spiral triggered by feeling trapped, either emotionally or physically. You drink heavily. You fall into a dark hole. And I take care of you until you get better. And then, we give you your sleeping pill and I take you home. When you wake in familiar surroundings, you slip back into the life of Savanna Portman."

She stares at me for a long minute. Then—

"This has been going on for years?"

"Yes."

"So why are you telling me all this now?"

"Because, Savi, I think we're in a lot of trouble."

FORTY-SEVEN

JACOB

Still kneeling in front of her, I find myself speechless for a moment.

My stomach churns with nerves.

I don't know if I can do this.

I don't know if I want to know the answer to the question that could change everything.

Selma paces behind me.

"Savi," I begin carefully. "You know about the man who was killed in the woods. And you understand that I—your *brother*—am the lead investigator on this case, right?"

She nods slowly.

"You know that several eye witnesses say they saw you that night. Also, I took a cast of the footprints found at the scene." A lump grabs my throat. "The tread on the shoes, as well as the size, match the pair you gave me."

I can see by the terror in her eyes, she already knows where I'm going with this.

I force myself to continue.

"The two witnesses—the gas station clerk and a man from the encampment—are willing to testify that they saw you that night." I take a breath. "And I'm guessing your minivan is on street cams, which will verify this. And tomorrow, the coroner is going to do the autopsy on Rat's body. His job is to confirm cause of death and to look for any trace evidence on the victim."

A tear falls down her cheek. She realizes where this is leading. I can see it—the pieces aligning in her mind. But I wonder if she's figured out the why.

The motive.

That part, I'm not ready to face.

Not yet.

So I continue.

"My job—my *entire purpose*—" my voice cracks "—is to find the person who stabbed Rat to death. To arrest them and turn them over to prosecution, where they will surely be convicted and sentenced to life in prison for first-degree murder."

A strangled sound escapes her throat. I reach forward, covering her hands with mine. My grip firm, grounding.

I lean in, lowering my voice, my words like a plea.

"Savanna, my dear sister—I have one question for you."

She meets my eyes, and for the first time since this nightmare began, I see something there that *terrifies* me. A flicker of doubt.

"Did you, Savi—or Quinn—kill Rat? Do you have *any* memory of that night? Anything at all?"

A long moment passes as we stare at each other. She begins to tremble.

"No... I don't know... Do *you* think I was Quinn that night? Did you see me, as Quinn?"

"Yes. I was gone, working, that entire night at an unreleased scene. When I got home early that morning, you—Quinn—were in the bathtub. On the floor next to you were muddy black clothes and a muddy pair of running shoes, exactly like the ones you gave me. On the console table were a pair of gloves and cinnamon gum. Hours later we gave you a sleeping pill, took you back to your house. You woke up as Savi and left for your big New York trip, not suspecting—or remembering—a single thing." My hands tighten over hers as if I can physically stop this from spiraling further.

"Savi, do you remember anything—*anything* at all from that night?"

Savi's face goes completely pale as she slowly shakes her head.

A wave of helplessness crashes over me.

I don't know what to say. I don't know how to fix this. Because how do you protect someone from themselves?

"Savi—"

"No." She jerks back suddenly, looking at me with wild, desperate eyes. "Tell me I didn't do it," she begs. "Jacob, tell me I didn't kill him. *Brother,* tell me I didn't."

I open my mouth but realize I can't say it.

Because I don't know.

Because *she* doesn't know.

Because I'm almost certain that the person I've been chasing through footprints and witness statements... *is my own sister*.

FORTY-EIGHT

SAVI

Suddenly, everything is too loud. The sound of my voice, my beating heart, my breathing, my own thoughts.

Jacob says something, but I don't hear it, because my chest is tightening as if someone has reached into my body and is clenching my lungs with their fists.

I can't breathe.

I try to say something.

"She's going into a panic attack, Jacob!" Selma's voice echoes through the blood pumping in my ears.

"Get her Valium. Quick."

Footsteps, rushing movement.

Time ticking.

The last thing I hear is:

"You're okay, Savi. You're going to be okay. You're safe," my brother whispers. "I'm right here, Savi."

And for the first time in my life—

I don't know who *Savi* is.

FORTY-NINE
JACOB

It's 2:17 a.m. when I finally cave and make the call.

The house is quiet. Savi is asleep, and Selma too. Finally. Katie called, concerned when Savi wasn't home. I told her everything, but asked her to hold off on visiting until tomorrow. Or, later today, technically.

Now I'm pacing the kitchen in the dark, lit only by the landscape lanterns outside. The phone feels heavy in my hand, like it knows this isn't going to be just another call.

Dr. Lin answers on the third ring, her voice low and groggy. "Jacob?"

"I'm sorry," I say immediately, rubbing the back of my neck. "I know it's late. I just... I didn't know who else to call."

A pause. I hear the shuffle of her getting out of bed. A lamp clicks on.

"It's okay," she says. "I've been expecting to hear from you again after you called me. I was worried that Savi might have been involved in the cabin incident. What's going on?"

"She knows," I say. "I told her. Everything. The kidnapping, the dissociative identity disorder diagnosis, the fact that she is both Savi *and* Quinn."

There is a long pause, then Dr. Lin exhales softly. "I knew she was at a crossroads; I told you. When I gave her the music box, the one you gave me from her childhood, I saw in her eyes that she was beginning to remember something, and that she might spiral. This call does not surprise me. How is she handling it?"

"The music box triggered a memory from the baseball park when she was kidnapped. How is she handling it all? She's unraveling. She doesn't know if she had anything to do with what happened that night in the woods. And... and I don't know what to do. I need advice on how to handle this whole thing."

There's no hesitation in her response. "Jacob. She needs to be in an inpatient facility."

"You know she won't go," I say, staring at my reflection in the dark window across the room. "The last time we tried that route, right before she was officially diagnosed, it broke her. It made everything worse. She felt trapped, remember? Cornered. She stopped trusting everyone—especially me. She *hated* me because I forced her into treatment. Just like the man forced her in his attic after he kidnapped her. And then her manic episodes got worse. That's when we agreed—when *you and I* decided to try something different."

I can still remember the day vividly. Dr. Lin and I sat in the back booth of Poppy's Diner. Sleet pelted the windows while thunder boomed in the distance. Thundersnow, they called it. It was like the world was ending. Savi had just refused to continue inpatient treatment, and I was at the end of my rope. She was unraveling by the day, and nothing we'd tried was working. And the worst part? *I* was part of the problem. I had become a trigger. I reminded Savi of everything she couldn't bear to remember—of a past buried so deep her mind had locked it away. That afternoon, Dr. Lin and I came to the hardest decision I've ever made: I had to step back. Not because I wanted to. All I wanted to do was protect my sister. But staying close was only making it worse.

So I let go. And then, not long after, Quinn emerged—her second personality—and Savi was officially diagnosed. Slowly,

Quinn erased Savi's childhood trauma from her memory—and that included me.

I'll never forget the first time Savi passed me on the sidewalk and didn't even flinch. Didn't look. Didn't blink. I wasn't her brother anymore—I was nothing but a stranger.

Dr. Lin and I both knew that forcing her into a facility again would destroy what little trust she had left. She needed support—but not the kind written up in clinical notes. She needed people. Familiar places. Predictability. Control.

So we built a different kind of net. A community net. And the whole damn town held it in place. I could never repay the citizens of Bear's Creek for how good they've been to my family, not in a million years.

"We decided we'd keep her close," I remind Dr. Lin. "At home. Safe. With a network of people who loved her and knew Savi was different, and needed extra help."

The truth is, only a handful of people in town know the full diagnosis—Dr. Lin, Katie, Selma, Chief Warren, myself, and the local law enforcement team. And they all have my direct line.

We set it up like clockwork. If anyone noticed something off— Savi in a location she doesn't usually frequent, Savi speaking like a stranger, Savi dressing differently, acting differently—they called me. Not the cops. Not the hospital. Me.

And they did. Every time.

"She's made it this far because of that," I say. "Because we let her live her life without locking her in a box and stamping her with a label she didn't ask for. You supported this plan; you said she could heal in her own environment."

"That was before *she knew*, Jacob," Dr. Lin says sharply. "Before she remembered the trauma and accepted the diagnosis. Everything's different now."

"She still won't want to go," I mutter, dragging a hand down my face. "And even if she did... she can't. She's potentially a suspect in a murder investigation."

"I understand," Dr. Lin says softly. "But this is no longer

optional. If she's remembering—if the walls between her identities are breaking down—then she's emotionally and psychologically unstable. You said it yourself. She's spiraling. If she doesn't get help soon, she's going to dissociate again. And this time, it might not stop with Quinn. Another identity could emerge. She could fracture further."

I grip the windowsill until my knuckles go white.

"I can't risk that. *She* can't risk that."

"Exactly," Dr. Lin says.

I release a long exhale. "I'll think about it."

"Please do more than that. Do what's right. For her." She pauses. "Jacob. Did you tell her *everything*?"

When I don't respond, she presses.

"Jacob. Did you tell her about that night?"

"No," I whisper.

"Because you think it's too much for her right now, or because you don't want to acknowledge the truth of what might be happening here."

"That one."

She's quiet for a moment. "I understand. Okay. I'm here whenever you need me Jacob," she says, the warmth in her voice returning. "But, please, Savanna needs treatment. Please, please, don't wait too long."

I hang up without saying goodbye.

I sink into a kitchen chair, lean forward, and drop my head into my hands.

My thoughts trail back to the final argument between us.

The last argument before she erased me completely.

FIFTY
JACOB

Seven years earlier...

Savi slams the car door before I've even taken off my seatbelt.

She storms into the house.

I kill the engine, sit there for a second, just breathing. Watching the snowflakes flitter against a gunmetal gray sky.

My hands rest on the steering wheel, but they're trembling slightly, and that rattles me. Because it means *I'm* slipping.

Because I don't know how to help her anymore.

Savi just told the doctor—her latest specialty therapist—that she didn't want to see her again. She canceled her appointments. She has officially denied treatment.

I follow her inside, slow and heavy-footed, like I'm walking into my own demise. The door clicks shut behind me just as she steps onto the staircase.

"Savi," I call after her.

She stops, but doesn't turn around. Her shoulders are rigid, her hands clenched at her sides.

"You can't keep running from this," I say softly.

When she finally turns around the fury on her face nearly knocks the breath from my lungs.

"Don't," she says, voice shaking. "Don't tell me what I can and can't run from."

"I'm not trying to—"

"Yes, you are!" she snaps. "You always are. You always think you know what's best for me."

I take a slow step toward her. "Because I *love* you, Savi. Because I've watched you unravel and rebuild more times than I can count, and I would do anything—anything—to spare you from one more break."

She crosses her arms tightly over her chest. "That's not love, Jacob. That's control. You control everything in my life. You even hid my keys from me the other night—that's crazy! You won't let me go anywhere without telling you—and don't think I didn't notice that you locked up your whiskey so I couldn't find it. You are *obsessed* with controlling me."

I stare at her, stunned. "Is that what you think this is? That I want control?"

She looks away, jaw clenched. But the tears in her eyes betray the defiant demeanor.

"No, Savi. That's not it. I'm trying to *help* you. But you see it as limiting you. You're projecting your childhood trauma onto me," I say gently. "I'm not the man who kidnapped you."

Her eyes snap back to mine. "I know that," she hisses. "But it doesn't change the fact that you never stop hovering. That you have inserted yourself so much into my life that I'm afraid to even date someone."

"Eric? Is that who you're talking about?"

"Yes. And don't even act like you haven't already ran a background check on him."

"I did. He's solid."

"Oh, well thanks for your approval, *Dad*." A red flush works its way up her neck. "Not that I care, because he's already asked me to marry him and I said yes." She lifts her chin. "You have to let me go, Jacob. You have to stop hovering. You watch me like I'm glass, like I'm going to shatter at any moment."

"Because I'm scared you *will*," I say, beginning to get mad myself. No, not mad. Frustrated. "Because you have. And every time, I've been the one picking up the pieces, Savi. Every damn time."

Her expression hardens. "Well, maybe I'm tired of being picked up. Maybe I just want to break and stay broken for a while. Maybe I want to figure out how to put myself back together without you swooping in to make it better."

That one lands like a punch to the gut. "You want me to stop caring?"

"I want you to *go*," she snaps. "You have a brand new wife. You're trying to start a family. Go live your life, Jacob. Stop trying to manage mine. I want you gone from my life."

"Is that what you really want?"

She doesn't answer right away. Her lips tremble, but then she nods, hard and fast.

"Yes."

Silence wraps around us. Heavy and suffocating.

I step back toward the door while sliding my hand into my pocket, around my phone.

"Go ahead," she mocks. "Go call Dr. Lin and tell her I've gone crazy—*extra* crazy."

I release the phone. That's exactly what I was going to do.

I pause by the door, and I try not to let my voice break.

"I'll leave you alone, Savi. If that's what you need. But I'll never leave you. Do you understand me?"

She doesn't move. Doesn't speak.

"I will *always* be watching over you," I say. "Even if you don't see me. Even if you don't want me there."

Her arms drop to her sides. She's shaking now, doing everything in her power to hold back the tears I see building behind her eyes.

"I'm your big brother. And there's not a single version of this world where I don't protect you."

I turn and close the door tightly behind me.

FIFTY-ONE
JACOB

The memory is so vivid that I can even remember the smell of the perfume she was wearing that day.

I lift my head from my hands and stare into the blackness outside.

A tear slips down my cheek.

I love my sister, so much.

And if she is innocent—and God, I have to believe she is—and if we can put this cabin murder behind us, then I'll do whatever it takes to get Savi the help she needs. Whether she hates me for it or not. Whether she ever forgives me or not. That doesn't matter anymore.

But even as I make the promise, my stomach twists.

Because there can't be an *if*.

I won't let there be. I will protect my sister, no matter what.

I will honor the promise I made to her so many years ago.

The tension in my chest has been a dull, growing ache all morning, but now, standing in the parking lot outside the coroner's office, it sharpens into something almost unbearable. I press a hand against my sternum, breathing through the pressure, knowing damn well it won't help.

I pull my phone from my coat pocket and call Selma.

"Is she still asleep?" I ask, watching my breath fog in the crisp morning air.

"She just woke up," she says. "Katie got here right after you left and is with her in her room. I'm giving them some space for now, then I'll make breakfast."

"Don't let her leave the house."

"Of course not, Jacob. But honestly, I don't think she'll want to. The woman just found out her entire life has been a carefully constructed lie and everyone, aside from her, knew about it. I can imagine that if it were me, I would want to hide under the covers for a very, very long time."

A selfish part of me is relieved that my sister is in no hurry to leave. Because as long as she's there, she's safe. Safe from the whispers that have already begun circulating. Safe from the police reports, the witnesses, the cameras. Safe from the very real possibility that she murdered a man in cold blood.

"Text me as soon as she comes downstairs."

"I will. Are you nervous?"

"Nervous that the coroner is about to find trace evidence on Rat's body that links to my sister? Yes. Yes, I am nervous as hell."

I glance at the building looming in front of me—a squat, gray-brick structure that looks more like a bunker than a public facility. No windows. Just thick, reinforced metal doors with peeling paint and a security keypad bolted beside them. A single fluorescent bulb flickers above the loading dock. I parked in the back lot, half-concealed by a hedge of overgrown cedar, hoping no one notices my truck here.

"No matter what happens, Jacob, we'll make it through this."

I don't say what we're both thinking: There is no "no matter what happens." Because there is no scenario where I let my sister be charged with first-degree murder.

After disconnecting the call I go round to the front of the building. Officer Woodson is waiting near the entrance, shifting his weight from foot to foot.

He looks like he's been waiting for me.

"Ah. I didn't see your truck back there." His voice is tight. "I need to talk to you. Two things, actually."

"Make it quick."

"It's out."

"What's out?"

Woodson rubs the back of his neck. "That your sister is a suspect in Rat's death."

The words slam into my chest like a bullet.

"One, she's not an *official* suspect, and two, how *the fuck* do they know that?"

"Probably from someone from the encampment. I wasn't the only one who saw Charles pointing and screaming that Savi did it. And I wouldn't be surprised at all if the gas station clerk also gossiped."

I jab a hand through my hair and begin pacing. This is the last thing she needs. The last fucking thing.

"Does she know?" he asks, his voice softer.

I swallow, nod.

"Shit, man," Woodson cringes. "I'm sorry. I can't imagine—I'm sorry. How did it go?"

"About as you'd expect."

"What did she say?"

"About the disorder? She's devastated. About whether or not she was at Rat's cabin that night? She has no clue. No memory of when she's Quinn. She has no idea if she killed Rat or not."

Woodson looks down. Neither of us speaks.

Finally, he clears his throat. "The other thing. As we suspected, street cams caught Savi's minivan outside the trailhead just after midnight. She's also on camera at the gas station before that."

"*Shit.*" I close my eyes, exhaling sharply. The evidence is quickly stacking against her, and I can't ignore it.

Woodson hesitates. "If she did it... why? She's never been violent before. *Quinn* has never been violent before."

"Right now, the 'why' doesn't matter," I snap. "The only thing that matters is making sure she doesn't get arrested for manslaughter." I grip the handle of the front door. "Let's hope to God nothing shows up on Rat's body that links her."

"Hey." Woodson catches my arm before I can step inside. "You know I've always looked up to you. I consider you a mentor and a friend, and I want you to know..." His gaze sharpens. "I'll do whatever I can to help you. I mean it. *Whatever* I can."

I don't need to ask to confirm he's referring to tampering with evidence to help save my sister from a life sentence.

I level him with my gaze and shake my head.

"Fine," he says. "But I'll be your ears. I'll let you know if anyone starts suspecting that *you're* messing with evidence."

I don't reply. I can't even think about that right now. So instead, I push open the door and step into the sterile, ice-cold morgue.

The odor of bleach, formaldehyde, and human decay is like a punch in the face. Always is, every time. Woodson grabs a jar of smelling salts from the vacant front desk as we pass by.

We step into the main room, where Dr. Mack Dempsey stands over Rat's body, naked on the metal slab.

He nods in greeting. "I'm still examining the stab wounds, then I'll cut him open. You guys are right on time."

My gaze flicks to the table saw sitting on the rolling table, then back to Rat. His skin is a sickly gray, stretched over his bones like wax paper. Stab wounds gape across his torso like tiny screaming mouths.

I stare at the macabre scene in front of me. I cannot imagine my sister inflicting this kind of violence on another human being.

Quinn, though?

Mack jerks his chin toward a counter lined with plastic containers and evidence bags. "I've already removed and recorded everything on him, if you want to take a look."

Woodson veers off, avoiding the sight of Rat's mangled body.

I force myself to focus.

This is just another case.

Just another body—

Until it isn't.

"Found something," Mack mutters minutes later. He flips down his magnifying glasses, leaning closer to one of the stab wounds. "Yep. A hair. A human hair..."

Woodson meets my gaze. I don't dare look at him.

My heart starts to race.

"...Definitely not his. Different color."

My stomach drops. The hair in Mack's tweezers is the same colour as my sister's hair.

I close my eyes.

This is it. This is officially the worst-case scenario come true. Now Savi will be asked to provide a DNA sample. But if she refuses, we'll have to get probable cause for a warrant. That buys me some time.

So I can make a plan.

FIFTY-THREE

SAVI

I wake up with—shocker—another headache. The duvet is pulled up to my chin like a shield. My limbs feel limp and drained, as if I've been wrung out and left to dry.

A dreary gray light seeps through the blinds making it impossible to tell if it's early morning or late afternoon.

I blink slowly, taking in my surroundings.

The walls are a deep eggshell, muted and soft, accented with delicate watercolors of sprawling landscapes. Cherry oak furniture anchors the space, potted plants adding touches of green. The bed is enormous, the mattress plush.

This isn't my house.

This isn't my bed.

Then everything hits me all at once.

Detective Lockhart—Jacob—my *brother*.

Multiple personalities.

Quinn is me. I am Quinn. I am both Savi *and* Quinn.

And finally, I might very possibly have murdered a man and not remembered doing it.

I curl my fingers into the duvet as my pulse spikes.

"Good morning, sunshine."

The voice is warm and instantly instills a sense of safety in me.

I turn my head to see Katie sitting in a chair pulled next to the bed, cupping a steaming mug of coffee between her hands. She looks tired. Her hair is pulled into a messy bun, her sweater loose and oversized, slipping off one shoulder. But it's her eyes that get me. The sadness and pity in them.

We stare at each other for a long moment, neither of us speaking.

A lump forms in my throat, and before I can stop them, tears well in my eyes.

"Why didn't you tell me? You're supposed to be my best friend."

Katie's eyes glass over with unshed tears. She sets down her coffee and moves onto the bed, pulling me into her arms. I don't even fight it. I bury my face into her shoulder, and begin to weep.

"Honey, I know," she murmurs, smoothing her hands down my back. "Let it out. Just let it out."

"I'm so glad you're here," I mutter through the tears.

"I wouldn't be anywhere else."

"And I can't even pretend to be mad at you. I understand why you didn't say anything. Jacob explained it all to me."

"I wanted to tell you, so many times. Believe me. But we all knew it would just make you upset."

"Well, you're right. I am very, *very* upset. Did you call Eric and tell him that I know everything now?"

She pauses. "No, I didn't."

"Good. Don't call him. Let me gather myself first. I'm sure he's been through so much with me already."

"When someone loves you, they don't look at it like that. It's just part of the journey. Honey, I know it's a lot right now, and that's why I'm here."

"*A lot?*" I pull back. "The whole town knows I'm crazy, Katie!" I grit my teeth and shake my head. "God, I feel like such an idiot."

"You're not crazy and you're not an idiot. Don't say that. Don't feel that way. This is just a little part of you. That's all. A little piece of the beautiful puzzle that is my best friend."

"A broken piece."

"A beautiful piece."

"Do you think I should tell my agent?"

"It might be good—healthy—to address it and face it head-on, but you can do whatever you want, Savi."

"I don't want to tell her. Not right now at least."

"I think that's a good idea. Let's get your feet under you first."

I nod, chew on my lower lip. "What if I become Quinn again? What are you going to do?"

Katie takes a deep breath. "When you research your condition, because I *know* you will, you'll find that almost every expert says that when you slip into your other identity, the best thing—the safest thing—is to let you be. So normally, I would roll with it. But now, with everything that's happened—"

"The cabin murder, you mean," I deadpan.

"Right. Now, I can guarantee you that if you slip into Quinn again, Jacob won't let you out of his sight. I promise you, between us, Quinn will never be left alone. Ever. Not anymore. We promise. We will make sure Quinn doesn't do anything that Savi wouldn't."

I exhale with relief. Then, "How can I believe anyone though? How can I believe Jacob? My whole life has been a lie."

Katie tucks a strand of hair behind my ear. "Jacob expected this question. He's got everything ready for you downstairs—your birth certificate, baby pictures, childhood videos, medical records. And Savi... remember, you grew up here. You can ask *anyone*. They all know you."

"Jacob told me that I was kidnapped."

"Yes. It was awful. My mom and dad even helped with the search."

"I don't remember any of it."

"I know, and I don't think that's a bad thing, really. Maybe it's a blessing. But everyone here remembers it, and that's why you are so loved and protected."

"It's like that movie," I whisper. "The one where the guy thinks he's living a normal life, but it's actually just a TV show and everyone is in on it. Everyone is pretending."

"*The Truman Show*," Katie says softly.

I nod. "Exactly."

A long silence stretches between us.

"Katie," I whisper, "do you think I killed that man?"

Her face crumples.

"If I did... why? Why would I do that?" A sob racks through me. "Am I evil?"

"You are *not* evil. Come here." Katie pulls me into her arms again.

Somewhere in the distance, I hear footsteps, then feel a presence lingering in the doorway.

"Give us a minute, please, Selma," Katie murmurs.

A pause. Then the sound of footsteps retreating.

I keep crying.

Katie keeps holding me.

And then, when I can barely breathe from the weight of it all, I lift my head, looking at my best friend with tear-streaked cheeks.

"Katie... *did I kill him?*"

She strokes my hair, her voice barely a whisper.

"I guess we'll find out soon enough."

FIFTY-FOUR

JACOB

The morgue doors creak open, and the moment I step outside, I'm blinded by an explosion of camera flashes. Beyond the light is a mob of reporters, locals, and tourists gathered to see what the commotion is about.

"*Detective Lockhart! Do you have a suspect in the Midnight Slaughter?*"

"*Was it premeditated or a crime of passion?*"

"*Have you made an arrest?*"

I should've expected this. Word travels faster than wildfire in Bear's Creek. The moment the town got wind that the coroner was conducting the autopsy, they descended like vultures.

The crowd presses in, camera shutters clicking, microphones shoved toward my face. Then, a single voice cuts through the chaos like a gunshot to the chest.

"*Detective Lockhart! Is it true the prime suspect in this case is the bestselling author—your* sister—*Savanna Portman?*"

The crowd goes silent.

I whip my head toward Andi Blake, the relentless journalist from the *Bear's Creek Tribune*. The one always sniffing around crime scenes, always first on the scene, first to report, first to twist a story into something unrecognizable.

Blind with rage, I advance, striding across the pavement with my fists clenched at my side.

"You didn't answer my question, Detective." Andi stands her ground.

She's been sniffing around Savi's story for years, frustrated that no one in town will talk.

"Is Savanna—who has a *long* history of mental health problems—the one who killed Rat?"

My hands are on her before I even process the movement. I slam her against the side of a news van, my fists gripping the front of her jacket, lifting her off her feet.

A collective gasp ripples through the crowd. The cameras flash like lightning, capturing the moment of Detective Lockhart losing control.

"Say her name again," I snarl, inches from the reporter's face. "And I swear to God—"

"Jacob!" Officer Woodson pushes through the crowd. "Let her go!"

"Fucking say it again, Andi." I shake her. "Say my sister's name again and see what happens."

Woodson's hand clamps down on my shoulder. "Jacob—enough!"

He yanks my fists down. Andi staggers, breathless, her eyes wide. But, like the blood-sucking journalist she is, she regains her composure quickly. She smooths out her coat, lifts her chin, and gives me a slow, satisfied smile.

"Jacob, *cool* it." Woodson steps between us. "What good are you going to be for Savi if you get thrown behind bars?"

The reporter brushes past me, turning to face the sea of cameras. "Well, there you have it, folks," she announces, tucking a strand of hair behind her ear. "Detective Lockhart declined to answer the question but became very emotional over it. So. Is his famous and mentally ill sister, Savanna Portman, the *real* killer? Make of that what you will."

The damage is done.

I push past them, shoulders tense, hands shaking.

Woodson follows.

I yank open the car door, slide inside, and slam it shut.

I peel onto the road, my head spinning with what has happened in the last thirty minutes.

One, a hair matching the same color as Savi's was found on Rat's body. Two, the town knows she is a suspect.

And now, thanks to my fucking temper, they all think she did it.

FIFTY-FIVE

JACOB

By the time I get to the station, the whole damn building is buzzing.

The front desk officer freezes, his eyes darting toward me like he's just spotted a grenade rolling across the floor. A cluster of uniformed officers loitering by the breakroom fall silent when I pass.

Ignoring the murmurs, I head straight for the chief's office.

His door is already open, waiting for me.

Chief Bill Warren looks up from his desk, sighs heavily, and gestures for me to come in.

"Close the door, Jacob."

The click of the latch feels deafening.

Bill leans back in his chair, the worn leather creaking under his weight. His weathered face is etched with concern, his graying hair a little more unruly than usual.

Bill is not just my boss. He's been a father figure to me for decades. And right now, he looks like he hates what he's about to say.

"Have a seat, son."

I remain standing, hands braced on the back of the chair in front of his desk.

I already know what's coming.

"What the hell happened out there?" He exhales, rubbing his temples.

"You saw the news," I say flatly.

"I did. I also got three phone calls before you even left the goddamn parking lot. The mayor, the commissioner, and the DA. None of them were particularly thrilled to watch my lead detective nearly strangle a reporter on live television. Good thing is Andi's not going to press charges. She got what she wanted."

When I don't say anything he sighs again. "Jesus, Jacob."

My grip tightens on the chair. "She went after Savi."

"I know. She's ruthless."

"She's a bitch. She said her name like it was a fucking death sentence. Like it was already decided."

Bill leans forward, folding his hands on the desk. "Listen to me. I get it. I do. You know how much I care for your sister; we all do. In small towns like this, we take care of our own. People are loyal to you, too. You've served our community for so many years, and everyone appreciates that, and that gives them even more incentive to care for Savi. The Lockharts are respected, no question about it —but that doesn't make it okay to slam a reporter against a van. You can't lose your head like that. Not now. Not when it matters most."

I sink into the chair, dropping my head into my hands.

The exhaustion hits me all at once.

"I can't let them take her," I whisper through my hands.

"I don't want that either." Bill says. "That girl's been through enough—more than enough. No one wants to see her in a prison cell."

I lift my face to meet his gaze. "Then don't take me off the case, like you're about to do."

"Jacob..."

"Chief, please."

"You know I can't do that. You're off."

My stomach turns to water.

"You're too close, son," he says, leaning back in his chair. "You know I should have taken you off the moment there was an eye witness account of your sister at the scene. But now? After today? There's no way in hell I can let you run this investigation. It's a massive conflict of interest."

"Don't do this," I whisper. My voice sounds desperate and weak. I can't stand it. I can't stand the way I feel right now. Like I have lost all control.

"I have to," he insists. "The whole damn town knows now that your sister is a suspect. If you stay on this case, every single thing you do will be called into question. Every decision. Every lead. Every piece of evidence. They'll say you're covering for her, obstructing justice. Hell, Jacob, you so much as breathe the wrong way, and you're going to give the prosecution a stronger case. You'd be doing Savi a disservice if you stayed on this case."

His words hit like a sledgehammer. I cannot believe what is happening.

"So what," I ask. "I'm just supposed to step back? Let someone else handle this?"

"I'll put Woodson in charge."

"You think he's ready for this?"

"I think he's got a clean record and no emotional ties to the case. That's what matters right now."

I stand abruptly, pacing. My pulse pounds in my skull.

This can't be happening.

This *can't be happening*.

"It's not fair," I mutter through gritted teeth.

"None of this is fair," he says. "Not for Savi, or for you. But it's happening."

My back is to him now, hands braced on the window frame, staring out at the cloud-covered town I've spent my whole life protecting.

"Has the murder weapon been found yet?" He asks.

"No."

"Good. It's hard to convict someone without the murder weapon. She's got that going for her."

I turn back to face him.

"I'm taking you off the case," he says, standing, his face softening. "But that doesn't mean you stop being her brother." He walks around the desk and places a firm, reassuring hand on my shoulder. "You're a damn good cop, Jacob. But right now? You need to be a damn good brother." He gives my shoulder a squeeze. "Now go home. Take care of your sister."

Before I step out, he calls after me.

"Jacob."

I pause, looking back.

"Whatever happens... I'm with you."

I nod once. Then, without another word, I leave.

FIFTY-SIX

SAVI

"Here, I brought you your laptop. Write."

Katie drops down onto the bed, jostling me from my fetal position. My eyes open and lock on the sunlight pooling onto the hardwood floor from the shutters she opened earlier.

"I can't."

"Bullshit. You're a writer. Writing has been a place of refuge your entire adult life. Write. Get it out. Maybe this can be a heck of a book someday. You *have* to get out of bed, Savi."

I sit up. The room momentarily spins as I pull my legs into a criss-cross. Maybe Katie is right considering the slightest movement sends my body spiraling. How long have I been in bed?

I take the laptop. "What day is it?"

"The day you're going do something other than lay in bed."

"I'm depressed."

"Me too. Get up. Let's be depressed together."

"Seriously, what day is it?"

"Saturday. You haven't left this room in two days."

"False. I went downstairs and cried over old childhood pictures."

"Stop it," Katie groans dramatically. "I can't take it anymore. Listen, you are not someone who gives up. And honestly? I think lying in bed and wallowing in depression only makes it worse." She nudges the laptop. "Write."

"I don't want to."

"Savanna Portman. I will pick you up myself and carry you downstairs if you don't get out of that bed—and we all know how that will turn out."

"Two heaps of broken bones at the bottom of the stairs?"

"Exactly."

"Fine." I pull back the covers and fling my legs over the bedside. My feet feel swollen and puffy when I set them on the cold hardwood floor. I'm still wearing the T-shirt, cotton shorts, and fuzzy socks Selma loaned me days ago.

Katie lays a robe around my shoulders. "Put this on. Your brother keeps this castle at a frigid sixty-five degrees."

I slide my arm into the robe—and I freeze in horror. Eyes wide, I slowly turn my head and look at Katie.

"Yes," she nods feverishly. "That smell is you. You stink."

"Oh my *God*." I sniff my armpits.

"Yeah, you haven't showered in, I'm guessing, more than two days."

"Should I... uh... shower first?"

"No, I'd rather you get your brain working, then I'll draw you a hot bath and I'll have wine, and you'll have tea."

"Where are you taking me?"

"Downstairs to the atrium. That room is a dream. We'll take the long way. Get the blood flowing in your legs."

Walking through the house feels surreal. This was my grandparents' home. Jacob and I grew up here. Being here over the last few days, I'm beginning to remember little things about the estate, fragments of a childhood that had been buried deep in the recesses of my mind. The hallways stretch wider than I remember, the air thick with the scent of old books, polished wood, and something faintly floral—a memory of my grandmother's perfume, though I can't quite place the name.

The furniture is grand, heavy, and expensive. I recognize some of the pieces.

My fingers trail along the edge of a table carved from solid walnut, its surface polished and gleaming under the sconces that line the stone walls. Suddenly, an image flickers in my mind—a younger version of myself sitting cross-legged on the floor, stacking blocks, my grandmother's voice floating through the air, warm and melodic. I remember how she used to call this table a "conversation piece," the kind of thing guests admired when visiting.

In the formal sitting room, I pause before an enormous, gilded mirror, its frame an intricate weave of gold-leafed vines. I see my reflection, but also something else—the faintest trace of a little girl twirling in a dress too big for her, laughing as it billowed around her ankles.

It's beginning to come back in slow drips, pieces of a life I had long forgotten.

A sudden burst of epiphany stops me in my tracks. "Oh my God!"

Katie startles beside me. "What? What's wrong?"

"If my grandparents were super rich, and now my brother is super rich... does that mean *I'm* super rich?"

Katie stares at me, then throws up her hands. "Finally! I've been waiting for you to make that connection for *days*, sweetheart. Yes, you're rich. Filthy, disgustingly, *generationally* rich."

I gape at her.

She grins. "And you know what that means?"

"What?"

"By proxy, quid pro quo, ipso facto—I, too, am rich."

My grin mirrors her own. "You didn't use any of those phrases correctly."

"No one knows how to use them, sweetheart, but I made my point."

A small, breathy laugh escapes me. It feels good.

Katie nudges me. "Okay, rich bitch. Let's get you set up."

The atrium is a dream.

The warmth of the glass room wraps around me like a blanket. Golden sunlight spills through the floor-to-ceiling windows, pooling across the plush rug beneath my feet. Lush greenery and cream-colored furniture fill the space. In the corner, there's a mint-green ottoman, a cozy loveseat, and an actual bird perched in the rafters, chirping lazily.

The air smells of brewed coffee, lemon, and something baking in the oven.

After settling onto the ottoman, Katie disappears.

I pull the laptop onto my lap and stare at the blank screen.

"Hi there."

I look up.

Selma stands in the doorway, holding a tray.

She's wearing a soft gray T-shirt and loose jeans, her long black waves cascading over her shoulders.

My *sister*-in-law.

"May I come in?" she asks gently.

"Of course. It's your house."

She crosses the room, setting the snack tray down on the glass coffee table.

"I'm so happy to see you down here." She settles onto the seat beside me.

"Katie made me do it. And uh," I wince, "sorry about the stink. I guess I've forgotten to shower."

Selma grins, then pushes up her pant leg, revealing a shocking stretch of leg hair. "Honey, I don't remember the last time I shaved my legs."

I laugh. A real, full-bodied laugh.

Smiling, she gestures to the tray. "I brought you water, coffee, and some lemon scones Katie baked yesterday."

"Thank you." I exhale. "And thank you for... everything."

Selma reaches for my hand, her eyes serious. "Listen to me. You are not alone; I just want to make sure you know that. You are not broken. You are so loved. And now? You know the truth. That's not a loss—it's a breakthrough."

His face is a wreck of bruises, cuts, and swelling. A thick white bandage wraps around his forehead, covering part of his brow. One eye is bloodshot, bruised, and grotesquely swollen. The brown suit I last saw him in is gone, replaced by an oversized Mercy Med Hospital sweatshirt that hangs loose on his frame.

I blink sluggishly as details come back.

The last time I saw my husband, we were on our way to dinner. We were fighting about me drinking while pregnant. Then—the car crash.

There are others in the room. Two nurses. One is older, mid-fifties, with tired, brown eyes. Her graying hair is pinned into a neat bun. The other is younger, blonde, with bright pink lips that are pressed into a thin line. A nurse in training, maybe.

They're both staring at me.

They exchange a look.

Something tells me that something is very, very wrong.

Andrew leans in, brushing my hair from my forehead. "Hi, honey. You're waking up. I'm right here."

"What's wrong?" My voice cracks.

Andrew looks at the nurse. A silent exchange passes between them.

"Can we have a moment?" he asks, his voice rough, wrecked.

The older nurse gently pats my hand before turning away, bowing her head as if in silent prayer. The younger nurse follows her out.

The door clicks shut.

Andrew turns back to me. His lips part, then close. His hand grips mine with cold, trembling fingers.

And that's when I see them. The tiny pair of purple leopard-print baby booties clutched tight in his other hand.

My chest caves in.

No.

My hand flies to my stomach.

"The baby." I whisper.

Andrew's eyes glisten with tears. "They did everything they could. It happened on impact. She didn't feel anything."

For a moment everything stops.

I can't breathe.

I can't move.

I feel nothing and everything at the same time.

"She?" I croak. "They—they know it was a girl?

Andrew nods. His fingers tighten around mine like he's trying to hold me together, keep me from unraveling right here in this hospital bed.

A girl.

I had a daughter.

Had.

Andrew swallows hard, his Adam's apple bobbing. "Lillian… there's more. You had internal bleeding. The seatbelt—it… ruptured everything. They couldn't stop it. They… they had to do a hysterectomy."

"What?!"

A knock at the door.

I barely register it. All I'm thinking is that I lost my child, and now will never have a chance at having another.

The same nurse peeks her head inside.

"He's here," she whispers.

A tall, lanky man enters the room. Thick silver hair. A black-and-white clerical collar.

"Mrs. Lockhart, I'm Timothy, the chaplain here. First, I want to say I'm so sorry…"

I stare blankly at the man as his words fade into nothingness.

"…and remember, she's with God now."

A burst of white-hot rage shoots through me.

She's with God now?

I *hate* him for saying that. I hate him for thinking those words would bring me comfort.

She's not supposed to be with God.

She's supposed to be with *me.*

She's supposed to be in my arms, breathing, and alive.

I turn my cheek away from the chaplain and stare out the window.

And there, in that moment, a part of me dies along with my baby.

FIFTY-NINE
SAVI

I wipe the tears from my eyes and stare at the chapter.

I feel Lillian's pain as if it's my own.

Why am I writing this? Why am I writing such dark things?

Why does *Quinn* want me to write this?

I lean back, angrily wiping my cheeks.

I need a break, so I leave the room and wander toward the kitchen. But as I near the doorway, I hear soft weeping.

I stop.

Katie isn't here; she left hours ago to check on the house and run errands.

It must be Selma.

I peek around the corner.

Sunlight slants through the windows, streaking across the stone kitchen floor. Selma is sitting at the breakfast nook. Dust particles float lazily in the air, suspended in the warmth. Her back is to me, shoulders shaking, her head buried in her hands. A glass of water sits beside her, untouched.

I watch as she slowly lifts it, takes a long, trembling sip, and sets it back down with a dull clink.

It's not water. It's liquor.

For a second, I debate giving her space. But then I think—if she wanted to cry in private, she could have locked herself in her room, or taken a drive, or done anything but sit here, in the center of the house, in broad daylight.

So I step inside.

"Selma?"

She startles so violently that she knocks over her glass. It crashes onto the floor, shattering into jagged shards. Clear liquid spills in every direction, seeping into the grout between the tiles.

"*Shit!*" she hisses, pushing back from the table.

"Stay there—I'll get it," I say, rushing forward.

I kneel down, carefully picking up the larger pieces of glass. The scent of alcohol rises up, sharp and acrid, mixing with the lavender dish soap rolling in the dishwasher.

Selma's face flushes with embarrassment.

"I haven't... I haven't drank in a while," she stammers, rubbing her hands over her face.

"You'll get no judgment from me—from either of my personalities."

For a beat, she just stares at me, then lets out a breathy, humorless laugh.

I toss the shards into the trash can, then grab a towel from the counter and wipe up the vodka as she lowers back into her seat.

"I heard you crying," I say gently. "Is everything okay?"

"Yes. No. It's nothing."

"It didn't sound like nothing."

Selma exhales, pressing her palms into her temples. "It's just... it's been a long day."

I glance at the half-full liquor bottle. "Want a refill?"

"More than my next breath."

Smirking, I slide the bottle toward her. "Then have the whole damn thing."

"Thank you." Selma lifts the bottle to her lips, and takes a long pull.

Once she sets it down, I say, "Now, tell me what's wrong."

"I had a miscarriage today."

The world slows. The last chapter from my manuscript barrels into me like the car that took the life of Lillian's baby.

Another *insane* coincidence.

Selma's chin trembles. "I was just five weeks, so it's not a big deal—"

"It *is* a big deal, Selma." I blink against the sudden headache forming between my temples. "I'm so, so sorry."

"We've been trying for years. This is my third miscarriage."

I drop to my knees in front of her, taking her hands into mine.

"When did it happen? Like, this morning?"

She shakes her head. "No. Right now. I went to the bathroom, and there was blood."

I squeeze shut my eyes. "Oh my God."

"That's why I was drinking. I haven't had a drink in two months."

"Have you told Jacob?"

"No." She shakes her head vehemently. "And please, don't. He's got too much going on right now."

"You mean trying to prove his sister isn't a stone-cold killer?" I deadpan.

Selma exhales a half-laugh, nodding. "Exactly." Then, her expression crumbles again. "He doesn't even know I was pregnant. Something in my gut told me to wait until I hit the two-month mark."

Before I can respond, the sound of the front door opening echoes down the hall.

Katie struts into the room, mid-lyric, her hair bouncing in a messy ponytail.

She stops cold. Her eyes flick from Selma's tear-streaked face to my own, then to the bottle of vodka sitting between us.

"Shit. What's wrong? Did we discover *another* personality?"

Selma and I both snort. So inappropriate, so Katie, and so—*so*—perfect.

Selma shakes her head. "I just had a miscarriage."

Katie winces. "Oh no." She crosses the room, reaching for Selma's shoulder. "I'm so sorry."

"Thanks. Please don't tell Jacob."

"Of course not." Katie hesitates, then kneels beside me, sighing. The three of us loop hands.

"Damn, life is hard isn't it?" she says. "You just had a miscarriage, Savi just learned her whole life has been a lie, and I'm a drunk who can't get sober or hold down a job."

We all stare at each other.

Then, one by one, we start crying.

Then laughing.

Then crying again.

At some point, Katie stands, takes a long drink of the vodka, then slams it onto the table with a dramatic flourish.

"There is only one cure for this godforsaken day," she announces.

Selma groans. "What?"

Katie grins, eyes sparkling with mischief.

"Girls' night."

SIXTY

JACOB

The house is dark when I slip in through Savi's back door, using the key Eric gave me years ago. I flick on the kitchen light.

Savi is everywhere. In the exposed brick walls, the pristine white cabinetry, the order of the appliances—each spaced precisely two inches apart. The copper pans that hang above the stove are stair-stepped to perfection, their placement symmetrical, intentional. Even the two matching barstools tucked neatly under the small island in the center of the kitchen, are positioned at identical angles.

My chest tightens as I take it all in.

Everything has a place. Everything has a purpose. Everything is arranged exactly as she wants it to be. My sister tried to control everything because her subconscious knew that ultimately, she had no control.

This house—modest but overflowing with warmth and comfort —is the life she has built for herself. A sanctuary free from the shadows of our past. Unlike the Lockhart Estate, which is steeped in history and burdened with memories we can never erase, this house is untouched by the trauma that shaped us.

And maybe that's what I've always envied about my sister—her ability to forget. The ghosts don't haunt her the way they haunt me.

"Okay, Savi," I mutter to myself, stepping farther into the kitchen. "What did you do with the murder weapon?"

I begin in the most obvious place—the knife drawer.

Sliding it open, I find the utensils neatly arranged in their designated slots. The expensive knife set I gave her and Eric three years ago is complete, each blade clean and accounted for. I run my fingers over the handles, my mind painting a picture of that night.

Quinn—manic, reckless, drunk—drives to the trails, stopping at the gas station on the way. The CCTV cameras capture her car turning onto Plummet Heights Road at midnight. Knife in hand, she hikes through the back of the woods, which she knows well, coming up on the cabin from the south...

I close my eyes. I still can't picture my sister doing such a savage thing.

Focus, Jacob. You're looking for the murder weapon—nothing else.

I move through the house, checking every logical place. Office, bedroom, bathrooms. I search the guest room, the attic, the crawl-space. Even the small utility shed in the backyard.

Nothing.

I step into the garage last.

Boxes are scattered everywhere. Some are open, items spilling onto the ground—books, clothes, old trinkets. Others are stacked haphazardly against the walls.

I frown.

This isn't Savi. She wouldn't leave a mess like this for days, let alone weeks. This is *Quinn's* doing.

I bend down and pick up an old newspaper. It's open to the last page where a column has been cut out of the paper. The headline reads: *Local Girl Missing for Two Days—No Leads in Ongoing Investigation.*

This column is about Savi, when she went missing, all those years ago.

My grandparents must have kept the newspaper, and later cut out the column so as not to upset Savi, and the remains somehow ended up in Savi's belongings when she moved out. There's no question in my mind that seeing this rattled *something* inside her.

I set it down, and pick up a picture of Eric. Dried teardrops blur the edges. I scan the disarray on the floor, my mind racing. Could this be a sign of a breakthrough? Of memories seeping back? A moment where her two identities were beginning to collide? Perhaps, in a haze of confusion, she started filtering through her past, not fully realizing why.

Then my eyes land on the small trash can next to the door. Inside, on top of everything, is a pink trash bag, the kind Savi keeps in the pop-up can that hangs from the back of her passenger seat.

I set down the picture and slide on a pair of latex gloves. I carefully lift the bag and undo the knot. Pushing past the used tissues and empty frozen yogurt cups I see a second bag. This one is a grocery bag, knotted at the top.

Carefully, I lift it out, cataloging the weight and shape of the single object inside.

My heart begins to pound.

With trembling fingers, I slowly untie the knot.

Tucked inside is a butcher knife, the blade and hilt coated in dried blood.

There it is.

I found it.

"Fuck." A rush of emotions slam into me.

There is no more ignoring what I've always known deep in my bones.

My sister did it—she really did it.

Quinn killed Rat.

I stare at the knife, my entire hand now shaking.

I'm holding the murder weapon.

The murder weapon. The one piece of evidence that could make this a slam dunk case against my sister.

I glance back at the oil stains where Savi parks when she comes home.

She didn't know. She had *absolutely no idea.*

After she killed Rat, after showing up at my house as Quinn, after I brought her back here the next morning, she woke up as Savi, having no idea a bloody knife lay in her van. She'd probably gone to run errands before leaving for New York City that afternoon, then saw the nearly full trash bag, pulled it from the car, and tossed it in the garage bin—completely unaware that she was discarding a bloodied knife along with her yogurt cups and receipts.

I close my eyes for a moment, inhaling deeply through my nose.

This is so, so unfair. It's unfair for my sister to spend the rest of her life in prison for something she did as someone else.

I stare at the weapon, my heart thundering against my ribcage.

The chief's words echo in my mind.

"It's hard to convict someone without the murder weapon. She's got that going for her."

He's right. Without a murder weapon, the case against Savi is circumstantial at best. They have the footprint cast, the CCTV footage, a possible hair, and witness statements—but those are all things that can be challenged, manipulated in the mind of the jury.

But a knife? A *bloodied* knife with her *fingerprints* on it?

They can't fight that.

I have two choices. Turn this in and let my sister be tried for murder.

Or make it disappear.

I look down at the blade one last time before knotting the bag again and turning toward the door.

SIXTY-ONE

SAVI

We've gone full slumber-party mode. Thick blankets are draped over the couch. An obscene number of pillows are stacked on the floor, creating a makeshift lounge area. Katie insisted on closing the curtains so the room mimics a movie theater. The only light comes from the flickering TV screen and the soft glow of a dozen scented candles flickering like fireflies in mismatched jars.

Pizza boxes sit open on the coffee table, their cheesy goodness competing with the sugary scent of vanilla cupcakes stacked on a tray beside them. Two empty wine bottles lean haphazardly near a pile of half-eaten snacks. A bottle of Dr. Pepper sweats beside me—full sugar, not diet. Not tonight. Tonight called for the real stuff.

We're halfway through a rom-com, laughing too loud at things that aren't that funny, pretending we're just three friends avoiding adulthood for a night. Selma and Katie are nestled into the blanket fort we made, thoroughly buzzed, passing a cupcake back and forth.

And I'm smiling. I'm laughing. I'm doing all the right things.

But inside I am a bubbling mess of anxiety.

I take another sip of soda and swallow hard against the lump in my throat that won't go away, like I can drown the thoughts down with carbonation.

The laughter beside me rises, and I echo it, though my stomach twists. It's like I'm wearing someone else's face. Someone more carefree. Someone who isn't unraveling by the hour.

A sudden chime breaks through the laughter. Selma straightens, reaching for the tablet charging on the side table.

I freeze, fingers tightening around my drink.

"What was that?" Katie asks, licking frosting from her fingers.

"Security alert," Selma mutters, tapping the screen. Her brows knit together, her expression turning serious.

A pit forms in my stomach. I set down my drink and sit up straighter. "What do you mean, security alert?"

Selma doesn't answer right away. Instead, she logs into the live feed of the outdoor cameras, pulling up a view of the massive stone gates at the front of the property. The second the image loads, my gut twists.

A sea of people is gathered just beyond the gates, on the far side of the road. Journalists, camera operators, photographers. Flashing bulbs flicker in the dimming light of dusk, casting eerie shadows along the stone.

Andi Blake stands at the forefront, just outside the gate—on the property—which triggered the system. She's speaking into a microphone, gesturing toward the house, her expression impassive but determined. We can't hear what she's saying. The crew behind her pans the camera toward the house, capturing every angle they can. The scene is overwhelming, surreal.

Selma inhales sharply. "Dammit. I thought we got rid of them."

"They've been here before?"

Selma nods. "The cops kicked them out earlier, but it looks like they're back. And that reporter is on our property this time. She's ballsy." She looks over at me and softens. "Don't worry. They can't get in. The gates are locked, and if they try, I'll call the cops immediately."

I nod numbly, but it doesn't ease my racing heart. I hate this. I hate that I'm causing so much chaos. That people I care about are being dragged into this media storm because of me.

Katie, now perched on her knees, watches the screen with narrowed eyes. "God, they're like vultures. Are they even saying anything new?"

Selma turns up the volume. Through the wind, we can barely make out Andi's voice.

"...sources confirm that local author Savanna Portman remains inside her brother's residence, refusing to comment on the latest developments. As we await further information from law enforcement, many are left wondering—what is she hiding?"

A fresh wave of nausea washes over me.

Katie huffs. "What a bitch."

"Has it hit national news?" I say, panic building.

"No." Selma clicks the screen off, setting the tablet down with more force than necessary. "That's enough of that. They can yell at the gate all night for all I care."

Katie, ever the enforcer of distractions, reaches for the remote and lifts it high. "Alright, no more checking cameras. This is a girls' night. No cameras, no reporters, no murder accusations. Just us and Barbie living her best life. Got it?"

Selma nods in agreement, reaching for her wine glass. "Got it."

Katie presses play, and the movie resumes, the bright, pink-hued scene filling the room once again. But I barely register it. Because deep down, I know there's no outrunning this. The time is coming.

I can feel it.

A deep, throbbing ache radiates between my temples.

I squeeze my eyes shut. *Not now. Please, not now.*

"I'll be right back," I mumble, pushing off the couch.

Katie and Selma are too caught up in conversation to notice me slipping out of the room. As I reach the hallway, I hear their voices lower, their giggles fading into something quieter, more somber.

They're talking about Selma's miscarriage again.

I think of my manuscript. Of Lillian losing her unborn child.

The headache spikes.

Clutching my head, I stumble into the kitchen. The overhead

light is too bright so I click it off. I bypass the glasses in the cabinet and shove my face under the faucet, twisting the handle. Cold water rushes over my lips, down my chin, shocking my system.

I grip the edge of the counter, swallowing greedily, desperate for relief.

Suddenly a kaleidoscope of images flash behind my eyes. Memories, I think. I'm *feeling* memories, like little hands trying to claw their way out of my brain. *That's* the trigger for my headaches—my body trying to remember something.

It's my memories trying to come back.

I cover my mouth with my hand, and again, hear the voice. *Quinn's* voice.

Just keep writing Savi...

I hurry into the atrium, now dark with night, grab my laptop, and power it up. The screen flickers to life. I click into my manuscript and reread the last chapter. The chapter I wrote of Lillian losing her baby—right before Selma lost hers.

Just. Keep. Writing...

SIXTY-TWO

TBD - A Thriller

Inspired by the mysterious Quinn and Jacob Lockhart of Bear's Creek.

Written by: Savanna Portman

Lillian

It's been five months since the car accident. Since a drunk driver stole our daughter's life before we ever got to hold her, and maimed me beyond repair.

The man who was driving the other vehicle had been driving under the influence of alcohol. He was convicted of negligent homicide and sentenced to ten years in federal prison with a $15,000 fine.

Andrew and I attend the sentencing.

We sit in the second row, our hands clasped so tightly my fingers go numb. In my naïve, desperate state, I think that watching the gavel fall will bring relief. That maybe, if I see his face pale when they read the sentence, I'll feel something—justice, maybe.

But instead, I feel hollow.

I don't cry. Andrew doesn't either. We just sit there, backs straight, bodies tense. We listen to the judge, to the attorneys, and we wait—hoping for an apology from the man who did this. It never comes.

Then, we walk out and drive home in silence.

The moment Andrew parks the car in the garage, I unbuckle my seatbelt, push open the door, and walk straight inside—to the liquor cabinet.

I yank open the glass door, grab the bottle of red wine we had been saving for our anniversary, and twist off the cork with my teeth.

Andrew doesn't say a word when he walks in. He simply takes the bottle from my shaking hands, pours two glasses, and hands one to me. Then, he guides me into the living room and sits down next to me, keeping the other glass for himself.

We stare into the fireplace that holds no fire.

"I don't feel any better," I whisper.

Andrew lays his hand over mine, squeezing tightly. His voice is raw when he speaks.

"Me neither."

"I still miss her."

"I do, too."

A tear slips down my cheek.

"I feel like no one understands because we never got to meet her. So why should we be grieving so much?"

"I feel that way too," he agrees. "How can I miss someone I never met? How is it possible to feel such a void in our life?"

"That's the thing, isn't it?" I say, my voice thick with emotion. "It's not getting better, it's getting worse. The missing, the wanting, the needing. The emptiness of it all."

That's what no one tells you about grief. That it never really fades. Instead, it constantly morphs into something else, manifesting in a thousand different ways. It's a deep dark pit that turns into a long black tunnel you walk through alone, knowing that there is no end. It's the exhaustion and fatigue that sits heavy in your bones, the kind that no amount of sleep, or food, or drink, or drug can fix. It's the rage that simmers just beneath the surface, the resentment toward strangers who smile too easily, who laugh without guilt. It's the way the sunrise offends you, how the birdsong grates against your nerves, how the sound of children laughing makes your throat close up. It's the bitterness toward well-meaning friends and family who tell you "time will heal" or "God has a plan."

I want to scream at them.

Don't tell me time will help.

Don't tell me medication will help.

Don't tell me to try to be happy.

And especially—*especially*—don't tell me that my baby would want me to be happy.

My baby would want to be *with me*.

I hate those people. I want to grab them by the shoulders, shake them, and make them feel this emptiness. Make them understand the unbearable weight of waking up every morning knowing your child is gone. *Forever* gone. And I'm still here. Without her. I have forty more years to pine over her. To crave her like something is trying to claw its way out of me. To wake up every single fucking day and remember, once again, that she's gone—*forever* gone.

I tip my glass back and drain it in three gulps.

"I think the thing is…" Andrew pauses to gather his thoughts. "I think we just have to sit in it."

"*Sit* in it?" I frown. "Sit in what?"

"The grief."

"What the hell does that mean?"

"It means we can't fight it. It's here whether we like it or not. Fighting it just makes it worse."

I blink at him, my frustration bubbling. "So, what? We just allow it to consume us?"

"No. We just… stop running from it."

I shake my head. "I don't understand."

Andrew stares at the empty firebox. His voice is quiet when he speaks again.

"Maybe if we stop chasing happiness like it's the be-all end-all in this life, like it's the entire point of existence, maybe we can finally just… be."

I start to respond, then close my mouth. My thoughts swirl around the idea that maybe the reason we're all so damn miserable is because the world—society, our culture—tells us that the entire point of life is to be happy. Hell, it's even written in the Declaration of Independence.

But how can we be happy with the constant suffering that comes with simply existing? Maybe the world has it all wrong. Maybe this constant pursuit of happiness is what's making us all so crazy. Maybe the expectation that life is supposed to be good is the very thing that's breaking us.

My eyes drift to the framed quote on the wall. One of Andrew's favorites. The one he hung in the study after the accident.

Let everything happen to you: beauty and terror.
Just keep going.
No feeling is final.

— Rainer Maria Rilke

I stare at it.

The thing is, I'm not ready to sit in my grief. I'm not ready to just *be*.

I'm too angry. Too unsettled. Too desperate for a way out.

I turn back to Andrew, boiling now.

"You know what's fucked up?"

"What?"

"The son of a bitch who killed our baby still gets to live."

"He's in prison, Lillian."

"Yeah, where he has a roof over his head, three meals a day, and a fucking gym," I snap. "And you heard the gossip—he'll probably get out early."

Andrew doesn't argue. He just watches me, his gaze steady.

"It's bullshit," I spit. "Why do some people die and others get to live? Why do the innocent suffer while monsters get endless chances?"

"That's one of the questions we'll never know the answer to."

"So it doesn't matter? The answer doesn't matter?"

"Does knowing the answer change anything?"

"That's not good enough." I shake my head, furious.

"It has to be," he snaps back.

I grab the bottle of wine, pour myself another glass, and storm out of the room.

I know, deep down, that Andrew is right.

But I don't care.

I will never be able to just *be* with my grief.

SIXTY-THREE

SAVI

I close the laptop, go back downstairs and tell the girls I'm going to my room to write a while before laying down.

Katie nods. "I'll be there in a bit with your sleeping pills."

The moment my door clicks shut behind me, I crawl into the bed, pull the covers over my head and sit cross-legged. The laptop hums as it wakes, the soft glow of the screen illuminating under the covers. Beneath the warmth of the blankets, hidden in my cocoon of fabric like a child sneaking screen time past bedtime, I begin writing—and I don't stop.

I type and type and type, like water breaking through a dam.

These words don't feel fictional.

They feel real.

They feel like memories.

Just keep writing, Savi...

So I do.

Feverishly. Desperately.

SIXTY-FOUR

TBD - A Thriller

Inspired by the mysterious Quinn and Jacob Lockhart of Bear's Creek.

Written by: Savanna Portman

Lillian

Andrew told me that the goal of grief isn't to find a way to make the pain disappear. It's about learning how to live with it better.

I am failing miserably at this.

It's been years since the accident. And even now, nothing is better. Nothing has healed. The grief is still here, heavy and suffocating, stitched into my skin like an invisible scar.

I don't think I will ever get better.

In fact, I think I'm losing my mind.

It started small. Forgetting where I put my keys, zoning out during conversations, little things I could brush off as stress or exhaustion. But then it got worse.

I wake up in places I don't remember falling asleep. I find notes in my own handwriting that I don't recall writing. Lists, reminders, sometimes just random words scrawled across the page that mean nothing to me.

I've lost fifteen pounds. I've cut my hair, then dyed it. I've thrown away my entire wardrobe, only to replace it with clothes in a completely different style—none of which I remember buying. I got a nose ring. Then I removed the nose ring. Bought a mountain bike. Rode it once. Donated it. My bathroom counters are littered with expensive skincare products that I don't need, my closet stacked with untouched books about grief and healing.

And the time—I keep losing time. Entire hours—sometimes full days—gone. I'll have no memory of it.

Then there's the voice. Not a literal voice, not like schizophrenia—at least, not the way they portray it in movies. It's more like a thought that isn't mine. Sometimes it whispers things to me.

You should wear red today.

Don't answer that call.

You're stronger than this.

The scariest part? Sometimes I listen.

I've been diagnosed with PTSD, severe depression, and a million other things it seems. I don't know—Andrew handles all my medical notes and appointments. I take a slew of pills a day, administered by my husband. Because, apparently, I forget to take them otherwise.

I forget because I *don't care*.

I don't even feel like a person anymore.

Most of the time I feel crazy, like I am detached from my own body. Like I am watching myself from a distance. Like someone—or something—else is taking over me entirely.

Little do I know, things are about to get much worse.

I'm curled up on the couch with a glass of wine when I hear the garage door open.

Andrew's footsteps are slow and heavy as he crosses the garage.

He opens the door, sets his briefcase down. His face is pale. His eyes wide and bloodshot.

Something is wrong.

"What is it?" I sit up, my pulse spiking.

His lips part, but no sound comes out at first.

"Andrew—what?"

"He got out."

My stomach turns to water.

We stare at each other.

For a long, deafening moment, I can't even breathe.

"H—how do you know?"

"Someone who works at the prison told me."

"They let him *out?*" I squeak. "Let him out of prison? *Why?*"

"Good behavior."

My jaw unhinges. "*Good behavior?*"

"I know," Andrew says, tears springing to his eyes. "I know, honey."

He crosses the room reaching for me, but I recoil.

I gape at my husband. My body begins shaking. "The man who killed our daughter... who *maimed* me... is *free?*"

"Yes."

I lunge at Andrew, collapsing into his arms. We fall to the floor together as a guttural scream rips from my throat.

SIXTY-FIVE

JACOB

The house is dark when I step inside. Only the soft glow of the kitchen light remains, where Selma is waiting for me. After I called her and told her I found the murder weapon in Savi's house, she insisted on staying awake until I got home.

Selma stands near the counter, wrapped in a thick sweater, her hair damp from a late-night shower.

I don't say anything. I just walk to her.

She meets me halfway, her arms wrapping around me, and we collapse into each other. She doesn't ask questions, doesn't ask for details. Instead, she cups my face and looks at me—really looks at me.

"One thing we can both count on through everything, all the uncertainty, all the ups and downs, is *us*. You and me. Okay? You and me."

Tears well in my eyes.

She kisses my lips, then, "Let's go. Let's do this."

Together, we slip out the back door.

The night is cool, the air ripe with the musty scent of lakeshore. A full moon hangs low in the sky, bathing the woods in a muted silver light.

We walk hand in hand down the winding trail toward the lake.

We don't speak.

The weight of the knife is heavy in my pocket, heavier than any piece of metal should be. The blade that ended a life. The blade that could end my sister's life if I let it fall into the wrong hands.

The treeline opens up and we step onto the dock.

A long, silver moonbeam dances across the surface of the water.

We step to the edge of the dock and look down. The water ripples beneath us, a dark, endless abyss.

Selma lets go of my hand and wraps her arms around herself, watching me as I pull the knife from my pocket.

I stare down at it.

It looks so ordinary. A butcher knife, stainless steel. The only thing that betrays what it has done is the dried blood on the hilt.

My stomach turns.

This is my sister's knife.

This is my sister's crime.

And I am about to erase it from the world.

A deep ache spreads through my chest. I think of my little sister curled up in bed, unaware of what I'm doing for her tonight. Unaware that I've chosen her over the law, over my duty, over everything I swore to uphold.

A part of me wonders if I will ever be able to look in a mirror again without seeing the man who covered up a murder. But I know one thing: I will always choose her.

My fingers tighten around the handle.

I take one last look at the blade. Then, I look at Selma.

She nods once.

With a deep breath, I throw the knife into the lake. It disappears beneath the water with barely a splash.

The ripples spread outward, shimmering beneath the moonlight, then fade into nothing.

Just like that, it's done.

"Come here," Selma pulls me into her arms. I bury my face in her shoulder.

"I love her," I murmur against her ear. "She doesn't deserve any of this."

"I know," she whispers. "And that's why you did this."

"And I love you, Selma." Tears spill down my cheeks onto her sweater. "So, so much."

I close my eyes, holding onto my wife as the cool wind brushes over the lake, carrying away the only piece of evidence that would leave no room for question in a jury's mind.

SIXTY-SIX

TBD - A Thriller

Inspired by the mysterious Quinn and Jacob Lockhart of Bear's Creek.

Written by: Savanna Portman

Lillian

I've been drunk since Andrew informed me that the convicted felon who ran into us was released from prison.

I've barely slept, and in the rare moments I have, I awake screaming, drenched in sweat. Every time my eyes close, the nightmare replays in excruciating detail—the blinding headlights, the impact, the way my head snapped to the side. Then, the sterile white hospital room. The look on Andrew's battered, swollen face. The words: *We couldn't save the baby.*

I jolt awake from another one of these night terrors, the sheet sticking to my sweat-drenched body. My hand flies to my abdomen. Where she *should* be. Where she *isn't.*

Breathing heavily, I rip off the covers. The cool night air sweeps over my heated body, making my damp T-shirt cling to my skin like paper-mâché.

Barefoot, I make my way downstairs.

Andrew is at the kitchen table, a nearly empty bottle of whiskey beside him. He's begun drinking heavily, too.

The dim overhead light casts deep shadows across his face. He's paler than usual, sickly looking. Another night with no sleep, I assume.

Andrew doesn't look up when I enter. He's used to my midnight rage. Instead, he rolls the glass between his fingers, staring blankly at the table like he's watching something invisible play out before him.

"I can't do this anymore." The words tumble from my lips.

Andrew doesn't react.

"Andrew, I said I can't *do* this anymore!"

Still, nothing.

Reeling, I grab the bottle, tip it up, take two big swigs, and slam it back down onto the table.

Andrew doesn't startle. He hasn't startled in a long time.

I slap my hands on the table, forcing myself into his line of sight. "We have to do something."

My feet move before I register it, pacing back and forth in tight, frantic strides. My hands tangle into my hair, nails digging into my scalp.

"We *have* to do something, Andrew," I mutter, over and over, my mind spinning, spiraling, until suddenly—

I stop.

"Look at me."

Andrew lifts his head fully this time. His face is sweaty, his eyes heavy lidded.

"We have to kill him."

Andrew blinks slowly, a deep frown forming on his face. "Wait— what?"

"The man who hit us." My voice sharpens. "We have to kill him."

Andrew exhales heavily, shaking his head. "Lillian… you're drunk."

"I'm always drunk," I growl, and begin pacing again. "And so are you! And neither of us are going to get better until we know he's gone. That he can never do to someone else what he did to us. That he can never kill another *child*."

"No, Lillian."

"It's not *fair!*" I scream, my voice breaking on the last syllable. "Our entire lives have been ruined and this monster gets to walk free? He gets another chance at life while our baby is dead? While I can never have another? If the assholes running the judicial system won't take care of him, *I will.*"

"Lillian, stop."

"No! It has to happen! It has to!"

"How?" Andrew demands, awake and fully present in the conversation now. "How exactly do you plan to kill him?"

"I don't know—I'll find him and I'll kill him. I'll do it for our baby. For her."

"And then what?"

"And then I'll be able to breathe again! And maybe—*maybe*—I won't wake up every goddamn night gasping for air because the nightmares won't go away. Maybe I won't need all these pills. Maybe I'll stop having all these ridiculous memory issues, maybe I'll stop going crazy. Maybe I won't feel like I'm rotting from the inside out!"

I am shaking.

I know I sound insane.

I *feel* insane.

I spin away from him, my hands pulling at my hair. "I don't care if I go to prison. I don't care what happens to me. I just need to know that he's gone."

Andrew stands abruptly, the legs of his chair scraping against the floor. "Lillian, *stop,* listen to yourself—"

"I am listening to myself! And I am finally making sense!" My voice ricochets off the kitchen walls.

And now I am sobbing. My knees buckle, and I drop to the floor at Andrew's feet.

Andrew kneels beside me, wrapping his arms around me and pulling me against his chest. I wail into his shirt, fists clutching the fabric with white knuckles.

I don't hear his short, ragged breaths at first.

I don't hear the faint, strangled gasping noises escaping his lips.

I don't notice that he's slumped forward against me—that it's no longer him holding me up, it's *me* holding *him* up.

His arms go limp, falling to my sides.

I pull back.

"Andrew?"

His face is as white as a ghost, his chest rising and falling in erratic, uneven jerks.

He clutches at his chest.

"Andrew?" I whisper, my voice hoarse.

His body convulses once.

Twice.

And that's when I finally understand.

He's not crying.

He's having a heart attack.

"*Andrew!*"

His glazed-over eyes meet mine, and in that moment, the last piece of my world comes crashing down.

SIXTY-SEVEN
JACOB

My headlights cut through the dark as I drive the long, winding road to Chief Warren's house. My knuckles grip the wheel, chest tight with the weight of what I've done.

I shouldn't be doing this. It's far too late. But after throwing the knife in the lake, and helping Selma fall asleep, I knew I wouldn't be able to sleep. Not until I speak to the only real father figure I've ever had.

By the time I turn onto the chief's gravel driveway, my head is pounding and I'm exhausted. The small, one-story farmhouse sits at the edge of a sprawling field, nestled between towering pines. It's the kind of house that just looks like home.

The front porch light is on, as it always is.

I don't even make it up the steps before the door opens.

Bill stands in the doorway, silhouetted by the warm light inside. He's wearing flannel pajama pants and an old Bear's Creek PD sweatshirt that's frayed at the cuffs. He takes one long look at me, and without a word, steps back, motioning me inside.

I swallow hard and cross the threshold.

The house smells like old leather and fresh coffee, even at this hour. The walls are lined with framed photographs of the past. Snapshots of the chief in his younger years, in uniform, at the station, shaking hands with former mayors and council members. But it's the mantle above the fireplace that holds the heartbeat of the man. A half dozen photos of his late wife, Mary.

Her warm, brown eyes gaze back at me from behind the glass, her smile as familiar as my own mother's. She was the kind of woman who made you feel like family, no matter who you were. Mary volunteered at the local school, and she used to sneak me and Savi cookies when were kids, and years later, she let me sit on the couch with a plate of spaghetti when I came over to visit the chief. When she passed, I sat with him on this very couch, drinking whiskey in silence until the sun came up.

And now, I'm back. Not for a funeral. But because I just destroyed evidence.

The chief exhales, long and slow. "Come on. Sit."

I lower myself onto the worn leather couch while he moves to the kitchen. The sound of cabinets opening and closing, the quiet clink of mugs, fills the space between us. He returns a minute later, handing me a steaming cup of coffee. I take it, grateful for something—anything—to hold onto.

Bill lowers into his recliner with a groan, rubbing his knee. An old injury.

He doesn't ask why I'm here. He doesn't need to.

He already knows.

"Bad night," he says, more statement than question. "I've felt it in my bones."

I nod, staring into the black swirl of my coffee. "Bad night."

He lets the silence settle—lets me be.

Eventually, I slide the coffee on the end table and then scrub my hands over my face. "I keep thinking about when I was a kid. How I always wanted to do the right thing. Be the good guy. The one who put criminals away. Got justice for people. But now... I don't even know what the right thing is anymore."

Bill leans forward, resting his elbows on his knees. His eyes, sharp and wise, lock onto mine. "Sometimes—*sometimes*—the right thing isn't always the legal thing, son."

"I found the knife," I say hoarsely, needing to say it out loud. Needing to confess. "It was in her trash."

I don't say what I did with it; he knows.

The chief exhales slowly, then leans back in his chair, rubbing a hand over his chin.

"There are times," he says, "we don't protect people because they're innocent." He looks me dead in the eye. "We protect them because they're ours."

I nod. "Savi's been through hell, Chief. You know that."

"I do. I remember vividly—searching for her when she went missing. I'd been on the force a while by then, but this was the first case that really shook people. Something like that didn't happen in our sleepy town. Not until then."

"I'm worried that this will break her. There are only a few things in life she has that keep her grounded."

"Like Eric. Does she still talk to him?"

"Every day, according to Katie. Katie told me she'll walk into the house, and Savi will be having a full-blown conversation with him, like he's standing right there next to her. It's been happening more and more lately. The other morning, Katie woke up and Savi was talking to him across the kitchen table. She'd set a coffee cup for him and everything. Katie said she looked so happy. She loved him so much—*so* much. She's never been able to let him go."

"And you haven't told her he died years ago? Not even after telling her about her disorder?"

"Absolutely not. Because to her, he's real, and he's an anchor in her life. Why would I take that away from her, Chief? It's beautiful. It's like their love has transcended time and space."

"Does she still try to call him?"

"Yes. Selma and I pay the phone bill for his number. It goes to voicemail." I shake my head. "Dr. Lin told me she's been having more nightmares about a man dying of a heart attack. So, maybe she'll remember soon. Maybe the memory is trying to come out. But for now, I want her to have that comfort. God, it's all so *unfair*."

"Yes," Bill agrees. "It is."

"But it doesn't change the fact that she killed a man."

The chief doesn't speak for a long time. When he does, his voice is softer than I expect.

"She's not the only one who's ever made a mistake, Jacob." He holds my gaze. "I've seen good people do bad things. Seen bad people do good things. Hell, I've been in this business long enough to know that nobody is all one or the other." He leans forward again. "You did what you had to do tonight. And I'm not going to sit here and tell you it was wrong."

I blink back the tears stinging my eyes.

"Tomorrow morning," Bill continues, voice firm now, "you're coming into the office."

I tense. "Why?"

"Because you need to be seen—cool, calm, and collected. The rumors are already flying, ever since your little incident with the reporter outside of the morgue. You need to be there—*in control*. You can't afford to be seen as compromised. Especially if, God forbid, the weapon is ever found."

I swallow hard, nodding.

"Okay." The chief pushes to his feet, stretches, then looks back at me. "Go home, Jacob. It's late. Get some sleep."

I stand and walk to the door, the weight on my shoulders feeling just a little bit lighter. And as I step out into the night, I swear I hear Mary's voice in the wind.

You did the right thing, son.

SIXTY-EIGHT
SAVI

Tears stream down my face. I am sobbing uncontrollably. My fictional character lost her baby, then her *husband* to a heart attack.

I feel like I'm spinning out of control. It doesn't feel like fiction anymore, it feels real. Like memories.

I glance at the clock then grab my phone and call Eric, needing to hear his voice.

It goes to voicemail.

Tossing the phone aside, I refocus on my manuscript, my finger scrolling wildly through the chapters. Like it has a mind of its own.

The pages stop scrolling once I hit Chapter One. The chapter that started it all.

Slowly, I re-read.

...My grip tightens around the knife in my hand.

It's time, the voice whispers, louder now.

Driven by some unforeseen but very real thing, I drop to my knees, raise the knife, and stab him through the trench coat.

Though his eyes don't focus, likely from the drugs lingering in his system, he jerks awake and looks directly at me. Shocked.

The emotion hits me like a tidal wave. The release of adrenaline is so severe that I'm suddenly dizzy, heady with a strange, all-consuming rush.

He moans loudly, and I'm enraptured by everything in the moment.

In awe of it. The suffering, the power I feel.

But as quickly as the emotion arose, a strange, counter-emotion collides with it— sadness.

No, keep going, the voice hisses. You have to do this.

Finish it!

When his body finally goes limp, the only sound left is my ragged, shuddering breath.

The knife slips from my fingers, clattering onto scarred hardwood floor.

I stare at the scene in front of me and rock back onto my heels, my chest heaving.

What have I done? Oh God, what have I done?

My fingers begin trembling as the weight of realization crashes over me like a tidal wave.

This isn't Chapter One.

This is the *final* chapter.

I yank my hands back from the laptop, like it's a poisonous thing. A headache spikes.

"Oh my God." The words on the screen blur in front of me, morphing from fiction into something raw, something real.

Something *I* did.

The air in the room suddenly feels suffocating. I scramble off the bed, running away from the laptop, running away from my words. I try to stand, but my knees buckle. I fall to the floor and grip the edge of the bed, my fingernails digging into the mattress.

Burying my face into the side of the mattress, memories pummel into me, one after the other. Images flashing behind my eyes like a horror film on fast-forward.

His face on the news. The headline: "*...local man known as Rat convicted of negligent homicide...*"

The newspaper article when he was released: *"Dewey 'Rat' Morrison, released early from prison, now a staple at the Halsey Trail encampment..."*

And finally, my voice: *"...if the assholes running the judicial system won't take care of him, I will. I will kill him. For her. For our baby."*

A sob rips from my throat, but no tears come. I am too stunned, too horrified. The final piece has clicked into place, and now I see it all, clear as day.

I remember now.

I did it. Lillian is me.

My manuscript isn't fiction. It's a *confession*.

The door quietly opens.

I turn.

Jacob's eyes are bloodshot, his face shadowed with exhaustion.

"Savi?" He frowns, taking in my panicked state. "What's wrong?"

I scramble across the floor and lunge into his arms, my body trembling.

"I did it. I killed him. I killed Rat. I remember now. I did it."

"Oh," Jacob exhales, squeezing tighter.

"My manuscript," I rasp into his chest. "It isn't *all* fiction—it's my story. I am Lillian. Andrew is Eric. It's my memory coming back, sneaking in through a fictional story. Most of it isn't real, but the big stuff is true. The accident, me losing my baby, me wanting justice. It's what happened to me. It's exactly what *I* did. I remember it now."

Jacob doesn't move, just holds me tighter.

"I did it," I begin uncontrollably sobbing, "and now I know why."

SIXTY-NINE
JACOB

I knew.

I knew all along why she did it. I just didn't want to admit it. I wanted to be wrong. Just like Dr. Lin suggested when I called her at two in the morning—

"Did you tell her about that night?"

"No," I whisper.

"Because you think it's too much for her right now, or because you don't want to acknowledge the truth of what might be happening here?"

She was spot on. I didn't want to acknowledge the truth. I still wanted to believe Savi was innocent. I didn't want to believe she killed Rat for revenge for what he did to her and her family, so long ago.

When Rat was released from prison years ago, Savi was in a more stable place. But then her career exploded—overnight success, book tours, interviews—and suddenly she was thrust into a spotlight she never asked for. The pressure built. She began to spiral. She felt trapped, disconnected from the identity she'd worked so hard to build. And in that space of unraveling, Quinn surfaced more than she ever had before. No longer quiet. No longer buried. She came to the forefront—and she wanted revenge.

Now Savi is unraveling in front of me. She's fought her way out of my arms and is pacing the floor like she might shatter if she stops moving. Her breaths are short and ragged. I reach for her, again, but she swats me away.

She has to get this out.

"I must have written about the murder right after it happened," she says, her voice cracking. "After I slipped back into Savanna. It was my memory screaming at me, trying to tell me what I—what *Quinn*—did."

She presses her hand against her temples. I know that headache. The one she's had since her career skyrocketed.

"All these coincidences between my manuscript and real life... it all makes sense now. They weren't coincidences. They were my memories coming back. Like when I wrote about Lillian getting fired..." She shakes her head, blinking rapidly. "It was my subconscious remembering Katie losing her job—over and over again. And Andrew's overbearing possessiveness of Lillian?" Her gaze finds mine, wide, frantic. "That was *you*. Your protectiveness. The way you always hovered, the way you never left me alone. I wrote it into the story because I was trying to remember."

I stand still, listening and feeling the weight of every word.

"Lillian fainting on the trail? That was me trying to remember the sickness I felt as I approached Rat's cabin that night. The headaches, it's all memories.

"The homeless man, Wally, who helped Lillian in the story..." Her voice falters. "That was my brain trying to remember Rat specifically. The goodness in Wally was my guilt and shame for what I did." She swallows, fresh tears spill onto her cheeks. "And Lillian's self-loathing, her poor self-esteem, her guilt—it wasn't just hers, Jacob. It was *mine*. I was reflecting on how I must have felt after my diagnosis.

"And finally, the fuzzy purple booties..." Her fingers dig into her arms. "They were mine. The ones Eric gave me after we found out I was pregnant. Before the crash. Before Rat drove into us and everything changed."

I remember that night like the back of my hand. I was at work, halfway through a long shift, when the call came in—a car accident, serious injuries, victims en route to the hospital. And then I heard my sister's name.

I ran through the station, out to my car, broke every speed limit to get to her, and when I got there, when I saw what was left of her —broken, bleeding, empty—I knew that nothing would ever be the same.

"I couldn't handle it, Jacob," she whispers now, her voice shaking. "The pain, the grief. Losing my baby, losing my ability to ever have another baby. And then—" Her hands curl into fists. "When Rat was released from prison, everything got worse. The rage, my medical condition. The injustice ate at me for years. The fact that he got to walk free while I was trapped in my own personal hell. I felt trapped, just like I felt when I was kidnapped so long ago." Her eyes burn into mine. "So I did it. I made a plan."

A single tear rolls down my face.

"All these years later..." Her voice is barely audible now. "I finally did it. I finally killed him. Revenge for what he did to me. To my family."

Savi shakes her head, stunned at her own words.

"It was right there the whole time, Jacob. In my manuscript. I was writing my story. My *confession*."

Her eyes drift past me, locking onto the doorway.

I turn to find Selma and Katie standing there, silent, tears streaming down their faces.

No one moves.

No one speaks.

The truth has finally been laid bare.

SEVENTY

SAVI

Once the sun fully rises, I insist on visiting my home. I'm not sure why. Maybe I'm searching for something—lost memories, pieces of myself I've yet to reclaim. Maybe I just need to stand in my own space, surrounded by things that once felt familiar.

Jacob goes first.

His truck rumbles down the long, winding driveway, as he heads for the iron gates. From where I sit, hidden in the back of Katie's car, I can already hear the chaos building—the media shouting questions, cameras crews getting ready to take their shots.

The moment the gates creak open, the crowd surges forward. Reporters press against the barricades, microphones extended like weapons, hoping to snatch even a fragment of a statement.

"Jacob! Jacob! Is your sister inside the truck?"

"Do you have a comment on the investigation?"

"Savi—are you guilty?"

Jacob doesn't slow down. He presses forward, his truck pushing through the crowd like a tidal wave breaking against a cliff. The reporters scatter, some running alongside, others shoving their cameras against his tinted windows, desperate for a glimpse inside.

And just like that, they take the bait.

The moment he's past the gates, the horde follows. Cars peel out, cameras flash as they chase after him down the main road.

Katie waits a beat, watching from the hidden back road that winds behind the estate. Then, she throws the car into drive, and we slip out the back.

I stay curled beneath the blanket in the back seat, my heart racing.

"We're good," Katie murmurs finally. "No one's looking at us."

I let out the breath I've been holding, and climb onto the back seat.

My phone rings.

Katie and I both jolt, the sharp vibration breaking the fragile silence. I fish it from my pocket and glance at the screen. Vivienne Hearst.

Impeccable timing—as always.

"It's my agent."

Katie's gaze lifts to the rearview mirror. "Shit. I bet it's hit the national news."

"What do I—"

"Answer it. Face it. Shit can't get worse. Might as well face it."

I snort, then exhale slowly before answering. "Hey, Viv."

"Savi. What the hell is happening?" Viv's sharp voice cuts through the speaker. "I just saw the news. Your name is being linked to a homicide investigation? Do you have any idea how big this is?"

I rub my forehead. "Viv, I—"

"No, no, listen to me," she cuts me off. "We can spin this. You're already a bestselling author, but this? This kind of media attention? It's every publicist's dream. We can turn this into a phenomenon. A mystery writer linked to an *actual* murder investigation? Jesus, Savi, this is *gold*."

Katie's mouth drops open. "Is she serious?" she mouths in the rearview mirror.

Viv barrels on. "The timing is insane. Your next book—your contract—the tour, the whole world is going to be watching you.

You need to capitalize on this. Tell me you're still working. Tell me you're already halfway through the next book."

Instead of feeling nervous, I feel angry. At her, at myself, at all the expectations. I understand now that the suffocating pressure to produce, to perform, to be something for everyone is what triggered my spiral. I felt trapped—just like when I was kidnapped.

I shift my gaze out the window. I don't know who I am anymore—but I know who I'm *not*. I know that being paraded around, shoved into the spotlight, forced to perform like Viv always wanted—it never felt like *me*. So maybe, because I don't know who I am, I can start here. I can start by rebuilding someone who *does* feel right. Someone who feels more like me.

I close my eyes, inhaling deeply. "Viv," I say, my voice quiet but firm. "I need a break."

"W—what?"

"I said I need a break. I'm sorry. I know everyone is counting on me, but I can't do this right now. I don't want to do the television show, and I want to cancel my contract with the publishing house —and with you."

Viv sputters. "Savi, sweetie, I don't think you understand how rare this opportunity is—"

"No, *you* don't understand," I interrupt, shocking even myself. "I am not an opportunity. I'm a human being. And right now, I need to step back."

Viv goes quiet.

Katie is grinning.

"Savi, this is a mistake," Viv says finally.

"Maybe," I admit. "But I've got bigger fish to fry at the moment."

I hang up the phone, and surprisingly feel just a little bit lighter.

SEVENTY-ONE
SAVI

Katie and I drive the rest of the way in silence, winding through the back roads of Bear's Creek, moving closer and closer to a place I no longer recognize as home.

We have to park nearly a mile away, on an old service road that cuts through the edge of the forest. With reporters camped out on the sidewalk in front of my brick house, there was no way we could come up the driveway without drawing attention. So instead, we hike in—sneaking along the wooded border of the property, ducking through thick brush, crossing the back lawn under the cover of trees.

No one notices us slip through the back entrance.

When I step inside, I feel like an intruder in my own life.

The late morning light filters through the sheer curtains of my living room, stretching across the hardwood floors. Everything looks the same, yet nothing does.

Because everything is different.

I reach into my pocket and squeeze the fuzzy purple booties. They haven't left my grasp since last night.

The door closes softly behind me, Katie's presence a warm anchor at my side. She doesn't speak. She doesn't rush me. She just stays close, like she always has, letting me move through the space in my own time.

My fingertips drift over the back of the couch as I take it all in. The familiar fabric, worn in places where I've curled up countless times with a book or my laptop. The framed photo of me and Eric on our wedding day. The blanket folded neatly over the arm of the chair. The candles on the coffee table, the little bowl of matches next to them.

I walk through my home like a ghost, touching the things I've had for years. The things I've arranged, the things I once thought defined me.

But I am not the woman who curated this space.

I am a murderer. And yet, I am also something else.

A survivor.

A sister.

A grieving mother.

A friend.

A woman who is finally beginning to remember.

I move into the kitchen, running my fingers along the cool marble of the island. The copper pots gleam in the soft morning light. Jacob gave them to me. My brother who has spent his entire life protecting me.

I lift a framed photo of me and Eric. In it, he's smiling. I feel like he's smiling at me, in that exact moment. Like he's proud of me, like he's telling me everything is going to be okay.

Smiling, I look at Katie. "I'll see him soon."

Tears spring to her eyes. "Yes," her voice cracks, "You will, sweetheart."

We turn and walk toward the hallway, my feet silent against the floor, and push open my bedroom door.

The bed is made, everything in its place. I move to the dresser, my fingers brushing over my jewelry box, my collection of perfumes. Everything is exactly as I left it—untouched by the horror of what I've done.

I turn to Katie, my eyes burning. "I don't know who lived here. I feel disconnected. Like I don't know who I am anymore."

She steps closer, her voice gentle. "You're Savi."

I shake my head. "No. I'm also Quinn. I'm Lillian. I'm a murderer—"

"You're *Savi*," she repeats, firm this time. "You are remembering. This means you are healing."

My chin quivers. I don't know if healing is the right word.

I drop on the edge of the bed, staring at my hands. The same hands that held a knife, that took a life. The same hands that, once upon a time, cradled my stomach and imagined a future that was stolen from me.

Katie kneels in front of me, resting her hands on my knees. "You are still you," she says, her voice unwavering. "Even after everything, you are still you. We will figure this thing out together, me and you, sister."

Tears slip down my cheeks. Because I know what has to be done. And unfortunately, Katie can't help me through it.

Not this time.

SEVENTY-TWO
JACOB

The moment I step into the station, I know something is going on. It's in the air, thick as fog, in the fluorescent-lit corridors. Conversations dull as I pass, the usual morning murmur shifting into hushed whispers behind my back.

Then I see him.

Chief Warren is waiting for me near the bullpen, his expression grave, his posture rigid. He holds a cup of coffee in his hand. Behind him, Officer Woodson glances up. Our eyes meet, and there it is—that look. The look people wear when they know something you don't but don't want to be the one to say it.

"Hey," the chief says, already turning toward his office. "Let's go in."

I follow, gripping my own Styrofoam cup so tight it nearly caves in.

Woodson remains outside.

The door clicks shut behind me.

Bill gestures toward the chair across from his desk. I don't sit. Instead, I stand there, heart pounding against my ribs, waiting for the hammer to drop.

Bill lowers into his chair.

"The hair found in Rat's wound is a statistical match to Savi's."

The Styrofoam cup crushes in my hand. Scalding hot liquid leaks into my slacks. I barely register the burn. Instead, I'm thinking about how I'd forgotten about the hair because no one had demanded a sample from her yet.

"Your DNA is in the system," the chief explains, handing me a pile of napkins.

I don't take them.

He sets them down and continues, "The DNA is a statistical match to someone in your family. Which means unless there's another Lockhart running around that I don't know about, it's Savi's hair in that wound."

My pulse spikes. "That's not enough—"

"It's enough," he cuts in. "It's enough for me to get a warrant for her arrest. And Jacob..." He hesitates, pressing his hands against his desk. "We've got more than enough for probable cause. You *know* that."

I feel woozy with a rush of emotion.

He continues, "The size of the boot prints found in the dirt around Rat's cabin match the size of her feet based on her height and weight. Her car was seen entering the road that leads to the opposite side of the mountain an hour before the victim's estimated time of death. The gas station attendant is willing to testify. Charles too. And now the hair."

My sister—my little sister, who I raised, who I swore to protect —is going to get arrested.

"The only thing we don't have," the chief adds coolly, "is the murder weapon."

A beat of silence stretches between us.

His gaze lifts over my shoulder, and his chin dips in greeting.

I turn just as the office door opens.

A woman steps inside. Slate-gray suit. Black heels. Short, sandy-blonde hair framing an angular face. There's intention in her step, and a sharp look in her eye. She carries herself like she doesn't have time for bullshit, and right now, I appreciate that.

"Jacob," Bill says, straightening. "I'd like you to meet Connie.

She's a defense attorney specializing in cases involving mental health."

I glance between them, still struggling to catch up. "I'm sorry—what?"

The chief leans back in his chair, rubbing his jaw. "I called her last night. Called in a favor. She drove down in the middle of the night."

I blink, trying to process.

"Mr. Lockhart," Connie says, extending her hand. "It's a pleasure to meet you. I think I can help your sister."

Her grip is firm and steady. Stronger than mine right now.

The chief gestures for us both to sit.

This time, I do.

SEVENTY-THREE

JACOB

Connie is calm and stoic, her hands folded neatly on the folder in her lap as if we're discussing a business deal, not my sister's future.

"Savi will be arrested tomorrow," Bill begins.

"Yes," Connie confirms. "The evidence is stacked, and the DA isn't going to hesitate." She lifts her chin, her voice steady but urgent. "Here's what's going to happen, Jacob. First, I need you to make sure Savanna is calm when they come for her. No resisting, no fighting. The worst thing she can do is make this more difficult."

"She won't resist." But even as I say it, I don't know if it's true.

"Good. When she's taken into custody, she'll go through standard intake procedures—mugshots, fingerprints, the works. After that, she'll be assessed by a medical professional at the station to determine her immediate mental state. Given her history, I have no doubt she'll be deemed a candidate for a psychiatric evaluation before trial."

I swallow hard. "Then what?"

"Then I'll file an emergency motion to have her transferred to a forensic psychiatric facility rather than holding her in general population at the jail. It's crucial we do this immediately, so she's not placed in a high-stress environment that could trigger another episode. I understand her episodes happen when she feels trapped. A jail cell will make her feel trapped and the last thing we need is for her to have a manic episode in holding—that could result in involuntary sedation or, worse, solitary confinement."

I glance at Bill. The thought of my sister alone, locked away in a cold, sterile room makes me sick. Bill dips his chin—*keep listening. Keep your head, son.*

"The forensic psychiatric facility will hold her for a period of evaluation, typically thirty to ninety days," Connie continues. "During this time, court-appointed forensic psychologists will assess her mental state, specifically whether she meets the legal criteria for insanity at the time of the offense."

"The legal criteria?"

She nods. "Insanity, in this context, means she was either unable to distinguish right from wrong or was acting under an irresistible impulse due to her disorder. Given her diagnosis of dissociative identity disorder, we can argue that *Quinn* committed this crime, not Savi. That she was in a dissociative state, disconnected from reality."

"So are you saying she'll be found *not* guilty by reason of insanity?"

"That's the goal," Connie says, her voice unwavering. "And if we succeed, she won't go to prison. She'll be committed to a psychiatric facility instead. Considering her notoriety and your pocketbook, probably a very nice facility."

"For how long?"

"That depends on a few things—her progress, the judge's discretion, the severity of the crime. In cases like these, I've seen anywhere from three years to indefinite commitment. But considering the victim's criminal history and the circumstances of Savanna's trauma, I have every reason to believe she won't serve more than a handful of years. I'm almost certain the judge will take it easy on her."

I exhale. I'm both sick and relieved at the same time. I recall Dr. Lin's advice when I called her in the middle of the night.

"She needs to be in an inpatient facility... If she doesn't get help soon, she's going to dissociate again... Do what's right for her, Jacob."

Connie softens. "Jacob, I know this is hard, but I need you to hear me. If we don't fight this the right way, she could be convicted and sent to prison for life. This is the best-case scenario. The alternative? She's in a maximum-security prison, surrounded by violent criminals who won't give a damn about her circumstances."

Bill leans forward, his gaze hot on me. *Keep your head, son.*

"Look," Connie continues. "When she's arrested, I'll be with her. I'll ensure she's processed with dignity, and that she understands what's happening. She will *not* be alone in this."

"And during this, what do I do? How do I help—what do I do?"

"You be her brother," she says firmly. "And you trust *me* to do my job."

I nod, inhaling.

"I know you don't want her locked up at all," she adds, reading my thoughts. "But trust me when I say this—as far as cases go, this one is a cake walk for me. Please know that. She'll be in treatment, getting help, healing. Probably in a beautiful facility. Also know, that in the majority of cases like this, where the accused finally snapped—so to speak—there almost always lies freedom from their demons on the other side. I know your sister has been fighting trauma ever since she was kidnapped, and what happened in the car accident only exacerbated her condition. She snapped, and maybe it needed to happen. Rock bottom is a very scary place, but it can also be the catalyst in recovery. This just might be Savanna's start at a brand new life, free of her demons."

SEVENTY-FOUR
SAVI

I wait until everyone—Katie, Selma, and Jacob— is asleep. Even the birds have gone quiet.

It's three in the morning.

I move slowly, deliberately. My breath is controlled, my heartbeat steady despite the weight of what I'm about to do.

I slip through the side door, the cool night air brushing over my skin. Quietly, I cross the driveway.

I pause. Look back.

The mansion looms behind me, bathed in the glow of the full moon. A house full of pain and trauma. Full of love.

A lump forms in my throat, but I swallow it down and turn away.

I slip into Katie's car, keeping the overhead light off as I ease the door shut. The soft click barely registers, but to me, it's deafening.

My fingers tremble as I shift into neutral, letting the car roll gently down the driveway, before pressing the ignition and driving to the back side of the property.

I don't need to worry about the security system, because I turned it off before stepping outside.

I glance in the rearview mirror one last time. Everyone in that house has sheltered me, protected me—even from myself. And yet, I know this is the right thing to do.

For the first time in my life, I *know*. Because Quinn would never do this. Quinn would never take responsibility, never surrender. Quinn would never turn herself in for murder.

But I am not her.

Not anymore.

Something deep inside me whispers that this—this moment, this decision—is the first step in finally addressing the trauma in my life.

I exhale, reach into my pocket and wrap my hand around the tiny purple baby booties. A ghost of a smile touches my lips as I feel the fuzzy fabric, the warmth of something that once was. My beautiful little girl.

Squeezing gently, I close my eyes and imagine her in little blonde pigtails, smiling. Her eyes are just like mine.

For you, I think, and then I press the gas and make my way into town.

Bolstered by a feeling of confidence and calmness that I can't explain, I walk up the station steps, open the door and step inside.

The officer looks up as I cross the tiled floor.

I stop in front of the bullet proof glass, tilt my chin, and jerk back my shoulders.

"Hello. My name is Savanna Lockhart and I have a confession to make."

SEVENTY-FIVE
JACOB

Courtroom B is stifling.

Or maybe it's just me. Maybe it's the suit jacket I'm wearing, the tie that feels like a noose.

Around me, whispers blend with the click of dress shoes, the rustle of papers, the occasional scrape of a chair leg against polished wood. Everything feels too loud and too quiet all at once.

Outside, it's mayhem.

National news outlets have picked up the story—*The Midnight Slaughter*. Satellite vans clog the courthouse parking lot. Reporters line the sidewalks like vultures with microphones, jockeying for the best camera angle, desperate to catch even a fleeting glimpse of *Bear's Creek's internationally bestselling author turned accused murderer*.

But Bear's Creek isn't having it.

The town has rallied behind Savi like a small army. Local diners are refusing to serve out-of-town press. The only hotel in town put up a "No Vacancy" sign last night, despite the fact that most rooms sit empty. The gas station clerk—yes, *that* gas station clerk—taped a piece of paper over the lottery display that reads: *We Stand With Savi*.

Even the baristas at the coffee stop are writing *Free Savi* on the coffee cups. Her favorite frozen yogurt store has a chalkboard out front that says, *Free muffins for fans of Holy Sheet Cake!* and *#SaviStrong*.

And it's not just locals.

Her fans have come out too—at least a hundred of them. Some drove in from neighboring counties, some flew in from other states. They line the edge of the courthouse steps with handmade signs that say things like *SHE'S A WRITER, NOT A KILLER*, and *I'd Kill For Cupcakes Too*, and *WE LOVE YOU, SAVI*. A few are wearing merch—T-shirts with cozy mystery puns and the cover of her book ironed across the front. There's even a woman in full Victorian tea shop cosplay holding a sign that says *Justice for Savi!*

My sister sits at the defense table, her hands folded in her lap. Her spine is straight, shoulders squared, chin tilted just slightly upward—not in defiance, but in acceptance.

She's wearing a simple black skirt and a soft gray cardigan buttoned to her throat. Her hair's pinned back, not a strand out of place. When she turns her head and her eyes find mine across the aisle—there's something new in them.

Clarity. Strength.

The woman sitting at the defense table is not the Savi who unraveled in my arms. Not the Savi who collapsed under the weight of things she couldn't remember. This Savi is calm. Grounded.

She's here to face what happened. And maybe, for the first time, she's not running from it.

And God help me, I've never been more proud.

Or more terrified.

Connie sits beside her, calm and unreadable, scanning her notes with a confidence that looks carved from stone. Across from her, the prosecutor, a narrow-eyed man named Byrnes, adjusts his glasses and turns toward the judge.

"All rise," the bailiff calls.

We stand.

Judge Martin enters—a woman in her sixties with stark white

hair and a gaze like a scalpel. Her presence silences the room instantly. She takes her seat, glances briefly at both tables, then nods. "Be seated."

The case is read. The charges are stated: First-degree murder.

My stomach clenches. But Connie doesn't flinch. She stands slowly and walks toward the jury box like she's known each juror personally for years.

"Ladies and gentlemen," she begins, her voice smooth and even, "today you're going to hear about a young woman named Savanna Portman. An accomplished author. A beloved sister. A survivor. And someone who, on the night of October 14th, experienced what the psychiatric community recognizes as a dissociative break resulting from a long history of unprocessed trauma."

She paces slowly, hands clasped.

"You will hear about the evidence—yes, her car was seen near the cabin. Yes, her footprint was found. But what you will not find is motive in the traditional sense. Not unless you are willing to examine motive through the lens of trauma. The lens of unresolved grief. The lens of a woman who, for years, had been living with dissociative identity disorder. A woman who didn't even know she had it."

She pauses, her gaze sweeping across the jury box.

"And if the words 'dissociative identity disorder' are unfamiliar to you, let me offer you something that is not. Savanna Portman was kidnapped at six years old. She was found three days later with no memory of where she'd been or what had been done to her. That girl was Savanna. And trauma like that doesn't vanish. It embeds itself, deep. Until one day, it erupts."

I glance sideways at Savi. Her chin remains lifted. Controlled.

"And years later," Connie continues, her voice growing firmer now, "a man, known locally as Rat, got behind the wheel of a truck and, while intoxicated, collided with a vehicle carrying Savanna and her husband. A crash that killed her unborn child and left her with permanent injuries. That grief didn't go away—it buried itself in her bones."

She stops at the center of the courtroom, letting the weight of her words settle.

"So, no—this is not a case about premeditation. It's not about revenge. It is about a woman fractured by trauma. About a part of her—an alter ego known as Quinn—who took over during an episode of dissociation and acted out the rage and grief that had been festering for years. *Quinn* is the one who acted that night. Not Savanna Portman."

She turns slowly, facing Judge Martin.

"The defense pleads not guilty by reason of insanity. We intend to prove that my client was under the influence of an irresistible impulse, triggered by her dissociative disorder, and that she did not have the capacity to comprehend the criminality of her actions."

SEVENTY-SIX

SAVI

Hours have passed since closing arguments wrapped. The jury filed out, and now we sit in the echoing stillness of Courtroom B.

The room is silent, but my thoughts are not.

They come softly now, not in panicked bursts like before. There's no racing pulse, no trembling hands, no dissociative fog pressing at the edge of my vision. Only a cool steadiness. Like the part of me that was always fighting has finally laid down its sword.

I sit with my hands folded neatly in my lap, back straight, chin lifted. I don't fidget. I don't glance at the gallery. I don't even blink when the heavy wooden door opens and the jury shuffles back inside. One by one, they file into the box.

Connie leans in. Her voice is soft, barely above a whisper. "It's time."

I nod. Not in fear, but in acknowledgment. Because I already know what they'll say. I'm not here to hope for an outcome. I'm here to accept one.

Behind me, I can feel Jacob's presence like a lighthouse through the fog. Steady. Protective.

"All rise."

The judge enters, robe sweeping behind her, followed by the jury foreperson. Her gavel is already in her hand.

She speaks with the gravity of a woman who knows this will make headlines. "The court acknowledges a plea agreement has been reached. The defendant will not be convicted of first-degree murder, but instead will be remanded to a psychiatric facility for long-term treatment under the provision of the insanity defense."

The courtroom erupts. Cameras flash, murmurers ripple through the crowd, fingers fly over keyboards. Someone cries out in relief in the back. I catch sight of a woman in a bright blazer scribbling notes, lips pressed tight in excitement. Behind her, someone is already on their phone, likely texting the headline.

But none of it bothers me.

"Miss Portman," the judge says, turning to me. "You will be committed to a secure mental health facility for a minimum of five years. You will be subject to regular evaluations and review. Should your condition improve significantly and your care team deem you stable, you may petition for release under supervision. Do you understand?"

I meet her gaze without flinching. "Yes, Your Honor."

Her gavel falls.

It's done.

Not just the sentence. Not just the trial. But the hiding. The fear. The pretending.

I'm finally telling the truth—even if the cost is everything. And for the first time in my life, I'm facing it.

Facing myself—whoever that may be.

SEVENTY-SEVEN
JACOB

Selma's hand finds mine. Katie is crying quietly behind me. I don't even realize I'm still holding my breath until my chest starts to ache.

I watch my sister—my brave, complicated, broken, beautiful sister—as the bailiff approaches. Savi turns without resistance, her head high. Shoulders square. She doesn't flinch when the cuffs click around her wrists.

And when they lead her out, she walks with a strange grace. Like a woman who's not just being taken away—but finally walking toward something that might save her.

The courtroom is emptying out when Connie corners me by the benches near the back. She's already shed her jacket, draped it over one arm, and pulled her hair into a quick twist. Even after what just happened—after securing the deal that kept Savi from spending the rest of her life in a prison cell—she looks sharp as a blade.

"I want to talk next steps," she says, cutting to the chase like always. "You have a minute?"

I nod and follow her into the hall, leaving Selma and Katie in the courtroom. The hall hums with excited conversation, the crowd cheers outside. It's chaos.

Connie guides me into a small conference room down the corridor and closes the door behind us. The noise disappears, a blessed relief.

She sinks into one of the chairs and gestures for me to sit across from her. "To recap, Savi was originally facing first-degree murder," Connie begins, folding her hands calmly. "But we negotiated a plea deal under the insanity defense statute. The court acknowledged her dissociative identity disorder, her extensive trauma history—the kidnapping, the crash, the fugue states. We presented airtight documentation from her old therapists, psychological evaluations, even character statements. It all painted a very clear picture."

I lean forward, elbows braced against the table.

"But that wasn't the whole play," she continues, her gaze sharp. "Savi isn't just another defendant with a mental health diagnosis. She's a nationally known author. A bestselling name. Her story's on every major news outlet in the country. That kind of exposure means optics matter—*a lot*. The DA didn't want the backlash of sending her to prison, not when the town's rallied around her and the cameras are rolling. So, instead of spending any time behind bars while things get arranged, she's being remanded to a secure psychiatric facility—the Harper House—effective immediately."

"*Immediately?*" My eyes pop.

Connie's smile widens. "That's right."

I blow out a breath and lean back. "Thank you so much; I can't thank you enough."

"I did my job. So. As we briefly discussed, Harper is in a long-term inpatient psychiatric facility just outside Boulder. Quiet. Private. High-profile clientele. The kind of place where celebrities go to detox and come out six months later with a book deal about the experience."

I exhale again, placing my hand over my heart.

"It's pretty much a five-star resort. But don't get me wrong. They do real work in there. EMDR, trauma-based therapy, dual diagnosis programs, one-on-one sessions, group work. It's not a vacation. It's accountability with spa water."

"How long will she be there?"

"Minimum five years," Connie says. "Possibly less with progress reports. Frankly? It's the best outcome we could've hoped for. This gives her a real chance to recover. To confront the trauma. To stabilize."

I nod, taking in adequate oxygen for the first time all day, it seems.

"She needs this, Jacob. I know you wanted to protect her—"

"I still do."

"I know," she says, voice softening. "But protection isn't always wrapping someone in armor. Sometimes it's letting them fall apart in the right place."

I look at the folder she pushes across the table.

A new intake form.

A new beginning.

Connie rises and collects her jacket, pausing before she opens the door. "You saved her life. You know that, right?"

I nod once. But I don't say what I'm thinking: I didn't save her. She did. Savi saved herself by telling the truth.

Even if it nearly destroyed her.

SEVENTY-EIGHT
SAVI

One Year Later...

Dear Quinn,

I never thought I would write this letter. I never thought I would find the words, or that they would ever be meant for you. But here I am, a year later, a different person—or maybe the same person who finally sees clearly.

I understand you now.

You were born from the darkest parts of me, a fractured piece of my soul trying to survive after a childhood that had broken us, and then later, an adulthood that devastated us. By holding my memories for me, you were my shield, my protector, my way of escaping the unbearable weight of trauma. You held the pain in your fists, the rage in your heart, the sorrow in your bones. I have hated you for that. I have blamed you for everything.

But now I see the truth.

You aren't my enemy. You were a survival mechanism.

Every reckless night, every drink, every headache—you were screaming for help in the only way you knew how. I see that now.

And God, I wish I had listened sooner. I wish I had been strong enough to face it all before it came to this. But I wasn't.

I want to thank you for being the part of me that refused to look away when I tried to erase our past. For being the part that made sure we survived, because without you, I'm not sure we would have.

I don't need you to leave. I don't need to erase you or shut you away like you never existed. You were always a part of me, and you always will be. And I think maybe—maybe you deserve to rest now. Doesn't that sound nice? Maybe we can learn to live together in a different way.

There is no rush, no timeline, no expectation for when, or if you'll take rest. Maybe you won't. And that's okay.

Because I forgive you, Quinn.

I forgive you for the things I once thought were unforgivable. I forgive you for the rage, the destruction, the chaos you brought into our life. I forgive you for the blood on our hands. I forgive you for being the voice that screamed when I stayed silent.

I love you, Quinn, and I am rooting for you. I will be the person we needed all those years ago. And when you're ready—whenever that may be—I hope you find peace.

I hope we both do.

Love,
Savi

SEVENTY-NINE
SAVI

I remove my reading glasses and rub my eyes. My latest manuscript glares back at me from my laptop screen—words still fresh, unfinished, waiting.

Releasing a long exhale, I take in the view outside my window. The sky is a pale blue, streaked with wisps of white clouds. A warm, late-spring breeze shifts through curtains, bringing in the scent of damp earth and wildflowers. Monarch butterflies, hundreds of them, dip between the hydrangea bushes below my room, their bright orange wings popping against the bright pink buds.

My gaze shifts to the empty crystal vase next to my laptop. Soon it will be colored with a single pink rose.

A smile crosses my face.

The door swings open, startling me. Katie breezes inside, balancing a takeout box in each hand. The scent of garlic and warm pita bread immediately fills the air.

"Hungry?" she asks, depositing the boxes on the small two-person table near the bathroom. "I only have a thirty-minute lunch today. We've got people coming in to tour the facility at one. Whatcha writing?" She squints at the screen as she pops open one of the takeout boxes.

"The same cozy baking mystery I was writing the last time you asked."

"*A Penny for Your Tarts?*"

"No, we decided against that title, remember? Sounds too much like farts."

Katie snorts. "That's right."

"It's going to be: *Curiosity Killed the Cannoli.*"

She laughs again. "Ah yes, that's right, the cat."

"Yes, the cute little tabby cat who eats evidence." Grinning, I shut my laptop. "Speaking of eating..."

I slide into the chair opposite Katie. We dig into our salads while she fills me in on the latest facility gossip.

"You will *not* believe who's checking in later today," she mumbles around a bite of food, wiggling her eyebrows. "Let's just say she had to cancel the rest of her international *music* tour..."

I laugh, shaking my head as my best friend dives into the juicy details of the latest pop star to enter the facility. We call it the Harper Club, because in so many ways, this facility feels more like a high-end retreat than a psychiatric hospital. Therapy sessions are intense and constant, but outside of that, we have freedom. After lunch, I'll join a yoga class beneath the towering oak trees on the back lawn. Later, I'll spend time in the expressive arts room, painting whatever my mind wants to release.

We have a gym, a library, a music room. There's even a barn on the property, where equine therapy is held three times a week. But beneath the beauty, this place is still a facility. A place where people like me come to mend, to unravel the knots of trauma, to find a way to exist without falling apart.

It's a beautiful place.

Next week marks one year since I arrived here. One year of treatment. One year of remembering. One year without any sign of Quinn. My (multiple) therapists say this is a very positive sign.

Maybe she's finally at rest.

I do hope so.

I have three more years in this facility until I am up for parole, though my lawyer thinks she can get me out after another year. Honestly? I'm fine either way.

I take a deep breath, sipping my iced tea.

I never thought I'd get to this place, mentally, emotionally, physically. I never thought I'd be okay.

But I am. Getting there, anyway. And if there's one thing I've learned, it's that healing can't be rushed.

Katie and I finish our lunch and she leaves in a hurry, eager to get back to the job that she's grown to love. And the best part is that everyone here loves her just as much. As the new patient coordinator, Katie gets to do what she enjoys the most: helps others. I have a feeling this job is going to stick.

Ten minutes later, I've just tied my hair into a bun when there's a knock at the door.

"Come in," I call, expecting Katie, hurrying back after forgetting something.

Instead, it's Jacob. And behind him, Selma.

"Oh my God," I gasp, rushing forward. "You're twice as big as last week!"

Selma laughs, cradling her growing belly. She glows, radiating warmth and love. "I'm officially down to one pair of pants that fit."

I wrap my arms around her, inhaling the faint scent of vanilla that always clings to her skin. She is my family now. She always has been. And soon, I'll be an aunt. I can't wait.

Jacob watches us with quiet affection. He's changed, too. Not long after everything happened, my brother left the police force and now volunteers at a children's safety center. Now he spends his days offering hope instead of chasing darkness. It's been crazy seeing the positive transformation in him. He is aging backward. He is finally happy.

Jacob walks around my room, inspecting it as he always does, ever the protective brother.

"When's your next checkup?" I ask, resting a hand on Selma's belly.

"Tomorrow. I think he's going to come early."

"Lockharts never do anything on time." Jacob winks, then eyes the bathroom doorframe. "You still good with the lock on this? It was a little loose last time I was here."

I roll my eyes. "Jacob. It's fine."

But I love him for asking.

Later that night, I'm curled up in bed, lost in a novel. The world outside is still, the kind of quiet that only exists in places of peace. A cool breeze drifts through my open window carrying the scent of honeysuckle.

A light knock on the door pulls my attention. I shut the book.

"Come in," I whisper, smiling from ear to ear.

My heart flutters as the door slowly opens.

Eric walks in, a smile on his face, a rose in his hand.

"You weren't going to sleep without saying good night, were you?" he whispers, quietly closing the door behind him.

"Of course not," I blush. "I always wait on you, my love."

Our eyes lock as he crosses the room, then leans down. Beaming, I close my eyes and lift my face to the warmth that is my husband as he kisses the center of my forehead.

"You still love me?" I always ask this.

"Every piece of you."

"Even the broken ones?"

"Especially the broken ones." His answer is always the same.

I nestle against his skin. "I don't care that you're not real," I whisper. "You're real to me."

"I told you." He taps my heart, "I'm always with you. Right here."

I take the rose from his hand—pink, always pink—shimmy out of bed and place it into the empty crystal vase I keep next to the window.

When I turn, a little head peeks out from the side of the bed. Shimmering blonde ponytails bob on each side, tied with bright pink bows.

My breath catches.

Eric smiles.

Tears swell as I rush to the center of the room, reaching for the little girl.

The little girl with eyes just like mine.

EPILOGUE
SAVI

The studio lights are warm, but not in an uncomfortable way. They glow softly against the backdrop of floor-to-ceiling bookshelves, giving the entire set a cozy, intimate feel. The audience is hushed, expectant, their eyes fixed on me as the interviewer leans forward in her chair, offering a practiced smile.

"Savanna Portman," she says, her voice smooth, warm, engaging. "You are once again a *New York Times* bestseller. Your latest cozy mystery, *Muffin but Trouble*, just hit number one on the list. You've cemented yourself as one of the most beloved voices in the genre. How does it feel, being back in the spotlight after so many years? After everything you've been through?"

I inhale, slow and even. My hands rest lightly in my lap, completely still. There was a time when questions like this would have sent my heart into my throat while my mind cycled through a thousand anxious responses.

But not today.

Not anymore.

I offer Gail a small, genuine smile, one that I *feel* rather than force. "You know... it feels good," I say honestly. "Better than good, actually. It feels right."

The interviewer tilts her head. "Right in what way?"

I take a second to consider my words. The past feels distant now, like an old story I once knew but no longer live inside of. I used to think I'd always be haunted by it, that Quinn would always linger in the background, waiting. But she's at rest now.

"It feels like I'm finally exactly where I'm supposed to be. I spent a lot of my life not knowing who I really was." I pause, glancing out at the audience, knowing there are people here who have struggled in their own ways. "But now, I know who I am. And more importantly? I like who I am."

There's a murmur of quiet agreement in the crowd, a few nods.

The interviewer smiles. "That's a powerful thing to say."

"It is," I agree. "And I don't take it for granted. I've worked really hard to get here."

Gail glances at her note cards, then back at me. "A lot of your fans have been wondering—why continue with cozy mysteries after everything that happened? Given your past, I think many expected you to pivot into darker thrillers, maybe something more psychological."

I laugh softly, shaking my head. "I thought about it, trust me. God knows I have plenty of content." A ripple of chuckles moves through the audience. "But, at the end of the day, I write what makes me happy. Cozy mysteries—these small-town whodunnits, these quirky characters, these fun and clever puzzles—bring me joy. Levity. And I think that's what really matters."

"So, no dark and twisted thrillers in your future?"

"No. I wrote a thriller once. It served its place in my life, and that chapter is closed."

I glance toward the side of the stage, where Jacob stands just out of view, arms crossed, watching with a small, private smile. He always comes to my interviews, and is still my greatest source of support—still my safest place. Next to him is Selma, holding his hand. Their little boy, Xavier, swings from her leg, totally oblivious, and wholly happy. Behind them stands Katie, beaming like a proud sister.

For so long, I thought peace was something other people got to have. Something I would always be chasing, but never quite reaching.

But now, as I sit here—confident, calm, whole—I realize I finally have it.

And I'm never letting it go.

A LETTER FROM THE AUTHOR

Dear Readers – let's stay in touch!

Sign up here to hear about my new releases with Storm:

www.stormpublishing.co/amanda-mckinney

Sign up here to be included in my personal newsletter:

www.amandamckinneyauthor.com/contact

If you enjoyed *The Perfect Murder* and could spare a few moments to leave a review that would be hugely appreciated. Even a short review can make all the difference in encouraging a reader to discover my books for the first time. Thank you so much!

facebook.com/AmandaMcKinneyAuthor

instagram.com/amandamckinneyauthor

tiktok.com/amandamckinneyauthor